"I Understand That Under Certain Circumstances, You Might Be Available....

"For certain kinds of work, I mean."

Gabriel surged to his feet. "Ma'am, I fly choppers. That's all. You got a hankering to tour the Everglades?"

Sarah Ann tried to smile, tried to remember this was all for Gramps. "I need you for a temporary assignment. I'll, uh, make it worth your while." She regretted the innuendo instantly.

He cocked one lean hip and absently ran a hand through his hair. "Just what exactly are you saying, ma'am?"

"Look, I've heard that you and your friends do...er, unusual work from time to time and I thought, that is..." She groaned in distress and buried her face in her hands.

"Spit it out, honey."

Lifting her head, she forced out the words. "I need a husband. Will you marry me...?"

Dear Reader,

Happy holidays from the staff at Silhouette Desire! As you can see by the special cover treatment this month, these books are our holiday gifts to you. And each and every story is so wonderful that I know you'll want to buy extras to give to your friends!

We begin with Jackie Merritt's MAN OF THE MONTH, *Montana Christmas*, which is the conclusion of her spectacular MADE IN MONTANA series. The fun continues with *Instant Dad*, the final installment in Raye Morgan's popular series THE BABY SHOWER.

Suzannah Davis's *Gabriel's Bride* is a classic— and sensuous—love story you're sure to love. And Anne Eames's delightful writing style is highlighted to perfection in *Christmas Elopement*. For a story that will make you feel all the warmth and goodwill of the holiday season, don't miss Kate Little's *Jingle Bell Baby*.

And Susan Connell begins a new miniseries— THE GIRLS MOST LIKELY TO... —about three former high school friends who are now all grown up in *Rebel's Spirit*. Look for upcoming books in the series in 1997.

Happy holidays and happy reading from

Lucia Macro

AND THE STAFF OF SILHOUETTE DESIRE

Please address questions and book requests to:
Silhouette Reader Service
U.S.: 3010 Walden Ave., P.O. Box 1325, Buffalo, NY 14269
Canadian: P.O. Box 609, Fort Erie, Ont. L2A 5X3

SUZANNAH
DAVIS
GABRIEL'S BRIDE

SILHOUETTE *Desire*

™ Published by Silhouette Books

America's Publisher of Contemporary Romance

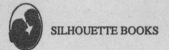

SILHOUETTE BOOKS

ISBN 0-373-76041-8

GABRIEL'S BRIDE

This edition published by arrangement with Harlequin Books S.A.

® and TM are trademarks of Harlequin Books S.A., used under license.
Trademarks indicated with ® are registered in the United States Patent
and Trademark Office, the Canadian Trade Marks Office and in other
countries.

Printed in U.S.A.

Books by Suzannah Davis

Silhouette Desire

SUZANNAH DAVIS

Award-winning author Suzannah Davis is a Louisiana native who loves small-town life, daffodils and writing stories full of love and laughter. A firm believer in happy endings, she has three children.

For my parents,
Lynn and Gordon,
and
for my kids,
Brian, Jill and Brad

One

As she parked in front of the bayside resort, Sarah Ann Dempsey trembled as before the gates of hell itself.

A humid gulf breeze blew in off Paradise Bay, exotic and perfumed, but offering little relief to the southwest Florida heat. Though only May, the coastline between Tampa and Fort Myers was already sweltering, and the little town of Lostman's Island was no exception. Beneath her practical gingham shirt, perspiration trickled between Sarah Ann's breasts, and she curled her sweaty palms around the steering wheel of her aged pickup, willing calmness.

Impossible.

But she had a mission. A desperate quest to ease an old man's mind, and no time for cowardice or feminine vapors.

"It's just business," she reassured herself. Slicking her dark hair back from her damp forehead, she automatically tightened her severe but sensible ponytail, then stepped out of the truck.

The marina had seen better days—and worse. Tall, clattering sabal palms shaded a weathered building, a combination business office, fisherman's supply and dining hall. White crushed-shell paths connected ramshackle, clapboard guest cottages. A wooden dock stretched into the sparkling waters of the bay, but the majority of the boat slips lay empty. For most of Sarah Ann's twenty-eight years, the Dempsey truck farm and orange groves had supplied fresh produce to this neighboring establishment. She and Gramps had watched the place struggle, then change hands—and names—again and again.

But the latest owners were something different. Mystery men, the gossips labeled them. A trio with questionable pasts, who vanished at intervals to pursue who-knew-what devilment, then reappeared to soak up the sun and rest on their laurels, caring little if the cottages were filled or the fishing boats rented.

As she opened the truck's tailgate, a delicate shiver tickled Sarah Ann's spine in spite of the heat. Making her deliveries, she'd seen them all at one time or another: the dark one, with the proud look of the Seminole; the Irishman with his merry grin and bleak eyes; and the one they called The Captain, tawny like a lion, and as commanding.

"Don't you dare lift them tomatoes!"

Sarah Ann jumped, her hands poised on the handles of the bushel basket holding the last of the season's crop. An Amazon wearing a man's rayon tropical shirt screaming with chartreuse parrots barreled toward her like a battleship under full steam. "But, Beulah—"

The woman batted Sarah Ann's hands away, lifting the loaded basket to her shoulder with no more effort than if it were a soap bubble. Her homely, corpulent face was ruddy with a high, indignant color matched by henna-red hair the texture of steel wool.

"Little gal, you'll bust a gut." A cigarette with an inch of ash dangled from Beulah's prominent lower lip, bobbing to punctuate her scolding words. "You ain't got the sense the Lord gave a lemming!"

"Sorry, I didn't mean—"

"'Sorry' don't pay the rent. Come in and get the last piece of chocolate pie. Rather you eat it as those no-accounts I work for."

Sarah Ann smiled, unoffended by Beulah's brusqueness. The cook-housekeeper had established herself at the resort as a force to be reckoned with, ruling the roost with her eccentric ways, sharp tongue and gourmet cooking. Now she was as much a part of the place as the salt water and saw grass, and as immovable. Nobody messed with Beulah, but over time she and Sarah Ann had developed something of a wary friendship.

"Thanks for the offer," Sarah Ann said. "But I'm not very hungry."

Beulah inspected her with sharp black eyes. "Been to the hospital?"

"Uh-huh."

"How's Harlan?"

Sarah Ann shrugged and looked away. It was difficult to talk about Gramps, but that's why she was here, wasn't it? Licking dry lips, she steeled herself for her task. "Is—is your boss around?"

"Who, Gabriel?"

Helplessly, she nodded. "I guess."

"What you need with that scoundrel, missy?"

Sarah Ann's face flamed. "Ah, it's a...personal matter."

"My, my, my. Hoity-toity, aren't we, now?" Beulah's pugnacious features soured. "Sure, sweet cakes, he's around here somewhere. Come on."

Beulah opened the screened door and led the way into a large open room with high pine beams and banks of screened windows. Serving as both lobby and dining hall, the area was furnished with shabby bamboo settees, Formica-topped tables and rattan chairs. Ceiling fans stirred the sultry air.

"Ain't seen him in the office all day. He's probably out there." Steadying the heavy basket with an arm as muscular as any All-Pro linebacker's, Beulah pointed through French doors that led to the cottages. "Help yourself. I got tomatoes to peel."

She disappeared through a set of swinging doors into the kitchen, her foam rubber flip-flops slapping an ill-tempered tattoo against the tile floor. Feeling abandoned at the other woman's abrupt departure and suffocated by the thick air, Sarah Ann wiped her damp palms on her jeans and tried to breathe.

How could she go through with this?

Plucking up her courage, she stepped outside. The compound was quiet except for the hum of insects in the scarlet hibiscus and purple bougainvillea that lined the paths. Sarah Ann glanced around, her resolve wavering. Gabriel wasn't here. Maybe this was a sign from heaven that she ought to abandon her desperate plan. Maybe—

Suddenly a rope creaked, drawing her attention to a pair of battered cowboy boots peeping over the harness of a hammock slung in the shade of two palm trees. Hesitantly, Sarah Ann moved down the shell path. The top of a blond head and two elbows came into view, followed by a swath of deeply tanned masculine chest laid open to the wayward breeze by an unbuttoned khaki safari shirt. Gulping, she stared at the man snoozing in the hammock.

His fair hair was thick and straight, sun streaked and cut short at the nape. Mirrored aviator sunglasses shielded his eyes from the glare but did nothing to disguise the square jut of a determined jaw or the deep lines of experience that bracketed a wide mouth. He was in his late thirties, she guessed, and his nose looked as though it had been broken more than once. It wasn't a handsome face, but forceful and somehow knowing, and to Sarah Ann the strength in it was intimidating. She was actually glad she couldn't see his eyes.

Her gaze flicked to the rest of him, and she drew an involuntary breath at the sheer masculinity on display, the width of broad shoulders, the flat muscularlity of his stomach, the light dusting of sandy chest hair that darkened as it traveled down his midsection. Fascinated, she watched a glistening pearl of moisture trickle from his navel and disappear beneath the low-slung waistband of well-worn jeans. From the length of his outstretched legs, she knew that he would dwarf her when he stood.

She also knew with an instinctive certainty that she was making a big mistake.

"You can waltz your butt right back where it came from, sister," a deep voice drawled. "I'm not budging."

Sarah Ann gasped, and shells crunched underfoot as she took an involuntary step backward. "Of course. Sorry, I'll go—"

He came to a seated position on the side of the hammock with the swiftness of a springing cougar and snared her wrist before she could back out of reach. Tipping his head, he surveyed her from her scraped-back hair to the tips of her old, canvas tennis shoes. "Who the hell are you?"

Shocked and chagrined, she stammered. "S-Sarah. Sarah Ann Dempsey."

"Dempsey? The folks who own the next place over?"

"Yes."

"Offered to buy a parcel of frontage from the old man a while back. Turned us down flat."

"I'm not surprised." Her heart pounding at both the suddenness of his onslaught and her own growing irritation, she lifted her chin and stared pointedly at his fingers pressing into her forearm. "Do you mind?"

He released her instantly. "Beg your pardon, ma'am. Thought you were someone else."

His voice held the faint twang of Texas, and his courteous reply was almost as unnerving as his pouncing on her. Surreptitiously, she massaged her wrist. "Ah, that's all right. I shouldn't have startled you."

"And I must be losing my touch. There was a time..." Grimacing, he dragged off his sunglasses. From his perch on the edge of the hammock, they were on eye level, and he speared her with a predator's tawny, golden-eyed gaze. "Something I can do for you, Miss Sarah Ann Dempsey?"

She drew a dizzy breath and knew she'd been right to be wary of those eyes. Yellow-brown, with a hint of copper ringing the irises, they seemed to see right down to the desperate center of her. Somehow she knew he was a man ruthless enough to use any advantage. Tongue-tied, she watched his patience wane.

"Ma'am?"

She pulled her scattered thoughts together with an effort. "Uh, you're the one they call The Captain, aren't you?"

Something in his expression closed down, and he scowled. "Beulah's been running her mouth, I see."

"No, that is—" She swallowed and tried again. "It's general knowledge."

"I'm retired," he said, his voice flat. "Just plain Gabe Thornton now."

Retired. From the military, without doubt. She found that encouraging. A man accustomed to giving and following orders, someone with the discipline to carry out instructions to the letter. Just what she needed. If he would hear her out.

"I understand that under certain circumstances you might be available." He lifted one sandy eyebrow in an unspoken question that caused her to stumble over her words. "For certain kinds of work, I mean."

He surged to his feet, and the hammock flapped, the sound raucous and harsh in the still afternoon. His expression was hooded, his eyes the color of melted caramel. "Ma'am, I fly choppers. That's all. You got a hankering to tour the Everglades?"

Squinting up at him against the brightness, she realized she'd been right about his height, for she barely came to his shoulder. It was all she could do not to take another step back. Instead, she shook her head, tried to smile, tried to remember this was all for Gramps.

"Nothing so spectacular. Just...a temporary assignment. I'll make it worth your while."

She regretted the innuendo in her words instantly, for he gave her another once-over, and his skeptical expression made her face heat with humiliation. Dammit, she knew she wasn't Cleopatra, knew she didn't possess a single quality that would turn a man's head, but she wasn't offering him *that!*

He cocked one lean hip and ran an absent hand through the damp bramble on his chest. Overhead, the palm fronds clattered. "What just exactly are you saying, ma'am?"

"Will you stop doing that?" she exploded.

"What?"

Shoving back the tendrils that had escaped her ponytail, she glared at him. "Ma'am-ing me to death! I'm not your sainted mother."

Incredibly, his lips twitched. "No, ma'am."

She blew out an exasperated breath. Damn him, he wasn't making this easy! She gritted her teeth. "I'm trying to make you a business proposition, if you'll only listen!"

His look was sardonic. "You've got my attention."

"Look, I've heard that you and your friends do... er, unusual work from time to time and I thought, that is..." She groaned in distress and buried her face in her hands.

A large hand cupped her shoulder, and his tone, though tinged with impatience, was almost kind. "Spit it out, honey."

Lifting her head, she forced herself to say it. "I need a husband. Will you marry me?"

She didn't look crazy.

But then, what did insane look like? Gabe wondered. Surely he would never have guessed it would be this bundle of female nerves currently gazing up at him as if he were the wrath of God Himself.

There wasn't much to her, either, except for a wealth of wavy raven black hair escaping from a childish ponytail. She was petite and too slender for his tastes, save the unexpected fullness of womanly breasts pressing against her simple cotton shirt. Her milky skin would never capture the usual Florida tan, and her features were even but insignificant, with the exception of her eyes, round and a blue that was almost violet. And she certainly wasn't any kind of sophisticate. Her hands were work worn, her nails short and practical. In any other setting, he'd have said she was as normal as the day was long.

No, she didn't look the type to propose to a total stranger, but what the hell did he know about such mysterious, unfathomable creatures as women? For the first time in a long and distinguished career, former Army Ranger Captain Gabriel Thornton could think of nothing to say. And Miss Sarah Ann Dempsey was waiting for an answer.

"Uh, ma'am—"

"Sarah. My name is Sarah Ann."

"Sarah." Frowning, he searched her face. "Uh, how long have you been out in the sun today?"

Frustration pleated her brow. "You don't understand."

"Damn straight I don't." He was coming out of his stupor, amazement and annoyance building to anger.

It was true he and his former commando partners, Mike Hennesey and Rafe Okee, were more or less free-lance troubleshooters these days and based their services out of the Angel's Landing Marina, so her roundabout talk of special circumstances and unusual assignments had sounded legitimate at first. After all, even tired old soldiers who'd found a home of sorts needed to earn a living. And they still had the special skills and training to do it on their own terms.

It was also true that he was punchy from a two-day-and-night charter flight carting biologists around the Big Cypress Preserve in search of some exotic endangered snail. It might not be quite as exciting as invading small subtropical countries, but he'd had enough of that to last a lifetime, and besides, it paid the bills.

So all he'd wanted was a little peace and quiet and some downtime in his favorite hammock. Certainly the last thing he needed was a madwoman flinging marriage proposals at him.

"Lady, I don't know what your game is—"

"I'm perfectly serious!"

"—but I'm not buying," he said, his voice a growl of warning. "You want a lover? Find a gigolo. A baby? Try the local sperm bank. In the meantime, I think you'd best sashay your fanny right off my property."

She blinked, taken aback, then burst out laughing.

Gabe was certain he was dealing with a lunatic now. Hysterical, that's what she was. Maybe Rafe's medical kit had some kind of sedative. . . .

"You actually think—?" She tried to stifle another bout of wild laughter and failed. "Oh Lord, I guess that was pretty clumsy. I can't help it. I'm nervous. I've never done this kind of thing before."

"That I can believe." Out of patience, Gabe grabbed her elbow and began hustling her around the front of the main building toward her parked truck. "Now, if you'll excuse me—"

"For gosh sakes, it won't be *real*." Her nose tilted at an indignant angle. "What do you take me for? I want to hire you to *pretend* to be my husband."

Gabe braked to a halt at her bumper, his boots sliding on the crushed shells. Somehow this admission was even worse. "Why the hell would you want to do a crazy thing like that?"

She glanced out over the glistening bay beyond them, chewing her lip. "I have my reasons."

"You'll have to do better than that."

Defiance darkened her expression, and a mulish pucker compressed her soft mouth. "It's about family. You won't understand."

Her assumption stung him. Hell, though he didn't see them often, he cherished his own family back in Texas. What couldn't he understand? "Try me."

She took a deep breath, weighing her words. "It's my grandfather."

"What about him?"

"He's dying. They tell me it's just a matter of weeks." Her eyes filled.

Gabe felt something punch him in the gut. "Damn, don't do that."

She leaned against the truck fender for support and blotted the corners of her eyes with her fingertips. "I'm sorry."

Feeling awkward around female tears, he began to stuff his shirttail into his jeans. "It's too bad. Crusty old codger, as I recall."

"Yes. He's all I've got." Regaining her composure, she lifted her face. "And he's worried about me. Wants to see me settled before he goes. It's become an obsession. He's not peaceful. So you understand why I'd do anything to make him happy."

"Even lie to him?"

She blanched, then swallowed hard. "Even that. What harm will it do?"

"I don't know. You tell me."

"None. And otherwise . . ." She broke off with a defensive shrug.

Gabe narrowed his eyes. There was something else, something she wasn't telling him. "Otherwise, what?"

"Nothing."

"If I'm going to even consider this, you'd better tell me everything."

Her head snapped around, her expression at once hopeful and full of trepidation.

"It's just that he doesn't think I can swing things on the farm after . . . after he's gone. He thinks if I don't have a man to take care of me, then he ought to sell the place now so I won't be strapped with all the responsibility."

"That seems sensible."

She shook her head fiercely. "No, he's wrong, but he's ill, and I can't convince him differently. I don't want to lose either Gramps or my home, Mr. Thornton. The Dempseys have been farming our land for three generations. I don't intend to let that legacy die."

Gabe rubbed the back of his neck, fingers automatically brushing the scar hidden beneath his hair that ran from neckline to ear. It was a tangible reminder of a nightmare of green hell and fire from his other life and more than enough reason not to complicate his quest for inner peace with some farfetched, off-the-wall scheme concocted by a lunatic!

"Ma'am—Sarah, this plan of yours is pretty drastic. And why me? Don't you have a boyfriend who could pull this off for you?"

A tide of hot color rolled up her cheeks, and her voice grew stiff. "No. At any rate, I'd rather keep this arrangement strictly business. You deal in unusual job assignments, don't you? No one need know anything about it except Gramps, you and me."

"You've got it all worked out," he muttered.

"There's really not much involved except your absolute discretion. Just meet Gramps a time or two, that's all. And I'll pay your usual fee."

She was so sure of herself he felt sorry for her. "Honey, you can't afford me."

Dismay widened her eyes. "Oh, but—"

"Believe me, you're out of your league."

"Then a trade," she offered, her expression harried. "That frontage land you wanted. I never meant to part with it, but if it's the only way..."

For a moment he was tempted. The land would offer better access to Angel's Landing, which was critical to keeping the enterprise afloat. But the whole setup was fraught with complications and headaches. No, better to follow his instincts. He shook his head.

"Forget it, I'm not interested. Not to mention that I have a real problem hoodwinking sick old men."

"It's shameful, I know that." Remorse quivered in her voice. "But it's for his peace of mind. You can't know how worried he is. If I can relieve that... well, I know God will forgive me this white lie. Please, Mr. Thornton. I'll give you the land."

"Not this time, honey." Shaking his head, he opened the driver's door and pushed her gently into the seat. " 'Husband' isn't my usual line of work. Tried it once. Didn't like it."

"It's not much to ask," she pleaded, as he slammed the truck door.

"Go home, Sarah Ann."

She leaned out the window, her eyes the turbulent blue of a thunderhead. "Why won't you help me?"

"I can think of about two dozen very good reasons."

"Name one," she challenged.

Goaded, he caught her chin between his fingers. "Try this."

Covering her mouth with his, he kissed her hard. Despite her smothered squeal of protest, she was surprisingly sweet. He held her fast, taking his time, savoring the spice and fury of her mouth. When he released her, she sputtered in incoherent outrage. His lips curled in a smile both wicked and satisfied.

"Let that be a warning, Sarah Ann. Little girls shouldn't play with fire. Every assignment gets my full attention. And real or not, *you* wouldn't like what I'd expect of a wife."

* * *

"What do you mean you turned it down?" Mike Hennesey wrinkled his sunburned nose and scrubbed at his russet curls in pure exasperation.

Rafe Okee sat across the dining table. Darkly bronzed and wiry, in jogging shorts, he pulled the bandana securing his long hair off his brow and snorted his agreement. "Hell, Cap'n! If this place is ever going to pay off, we need that frontage—bad."

Freshly showered and looking forward to a quiet meal, Gabe scowled at his partners' attack, then turned a fierce glare at the true author of this situation. "Been spilling the beans again, Beulah?"

"All I said was, it's a damn fool who cuts off his nose to spite his face."

With a graceful agility belied by her size and bulk, she slid the three plates she held balanced on one arm onto the table in front of the three men. Somehow she even managed to accomplish this feat without dripping any cigarette ashes in the dishes.

Grilled jumbo shrimp sizzled on the gargantuan platters, filling the evening air with a tantalizing aroma, but Gabe was in no mood to be placated by Beulah's culinary skills, not when she'd obviously been indulging in her favorite hobby—troublemaking.

"You got a long nose, Beulah. That was a private conversation."

She gave a laugh that sounded like a caw. "Cat fight was more like it. Heard you all the way to Tampa, I'll bet. That gal sure left out of here steamed up."

"Oh, hell, Gabe!" Mike groaned. "What'd you do to her?"

"You don't want to know," Beulah said, smirking. "It wasn't pretty."

"Don't you have something better to do?" Gabe demanded.

"Don't take that tone with me, mister." Growling under her breath, she stomped toward the kitchen.

"Jeez, did you have to tick her off again?" Rafe asked in disgust. "We'll be eating kibbles for a week."

"I don't know why we put up with that Medusa." Gabe swung a leg over his chair.

"Yes, you do." Mike bit into a shrimp and gave a long, appreciative sigh. "And this is it."

Rafe eyed his former commanding officer belligerently. "What I want to know is, if old man Dempsey was so willing to deal on that property that he sent his own granddaughter over to talk to you, why didn't you latch it down, pronto?"

Gabe shifted in his seat. "The, uh, price was too high."

Miracle of miracles, apparently Beulah hadn't overheard Sarah Ann's outlandish proposal and passed that on, too. At least the poor girl would be spared that kind of ridicule and embarrassment. That he would take an unmerciful ribbing from his partners didn't even enter into it, of course.

"Heck, Gabe, we need that frontage at any price," Mike said. "I didn't invest in this joint just to go bankrupt."

"We're far from that," he protested, picking up his fork. "Besides, what are you complaining about? You're hardly around a week per month these days."

Mike grimaced. "Yeah, finding missing persons turns out to be a booming business."

"Well, that last search-and-rescue nearly killed me. I'm getting too old for the Special Ops game," Rafe groused.

"You got a better idea?"

"Sure. Improve access to Angel's Landing, advertise and put up that RV park like we talked about, so we can make this place pay for itself and all retire."

Mike pushed his empty plate aside and grinned. "I thought we'd done that already."

"Mothballing the uniforms was only part of it," Gabe pointed out.

The Fallen Angels team had served well together through dangerous times, in situations no government would even admit to knowing about. But a man's psyche could only take so much. One by one, they'd reached a saturation point when they'd each seen and done too much to stay any longer.

When Rafe found this place and offered a third interest to his closest buddies, Gabe immediately came aboard. He'd been drifting aimlessly—South America, the Far East, it didn't matter—too soul weary to go home to Texas, too battle-scarred to fit in anywhere else. The partnership was a godsend, a chance to reconnect to life. And it was working. There was healing in the hard physical work, the goals, the friendship. The three of them were bound by bonds of blood, camaraderie and loyalty. They didn't let each other down.

Gabe grimaced. Only he had, by letting his temper get the best of him and scaring off Miss Sarah Ann Dempsey and their best chance at that property.

"Can't say that I miss those fatigues, you know. I still break out in hives whenever I see khaki." Joking, Mike's grin grew even wider. "And at least we don't have to salute Gabe anymore."

"No, we can give *him* orders now," Rafe said.

Gabe's mouth twitched. "Mutiny, is it?"

"Since you obviously screwed up earlier, you get to re-peat the assignment." Rafe jabbed a finger at him. "Get in touch with Miss Dempsey and open negotiations again. *Sir.*"

Gabe's belly clenched, and he frowned. "Waste of time."

"That bad, huh?"

"Hey, Mike's the ladies' man in the outfit, remember?"

The Irishman laughed. "You're saying you didn't handle things with your usual finesse and flair?"

"Something like that."

Rafe shrugged. "Tough. Get back in that ring and start swinging. A Ranger never admits defeat."

"I really blew it," Gabe admitted. "One look at me, and she'll spit in my eye."

Mike and Rafe glanced at each other. Grinned.

"So, *duck,* sir."

Two

———

Little girl...

Sarah Ann folded Gramps's pajama top with a savage snap of her wrists.

Out of your league...

Her face burned. The arrogance. The utter gall!

Try this...

Teeth gritted, she slapped the pj's onto the bureau, then cast an anxious look at the wizened man asleep in the hospital bed. The window blinds were closed against the glare of a lingering sunset and the room was dim, illuminated only by the pale light of the fluorescent fixture above the narrow bed. Silver stubble sprouted on Harlan Dempsey's weathered cheeks, and the IV tube dripped quietly into a thin arm, but he didn't stir.

Sarah Ann drew a deep breath, wrinkling her nose at the familiar scents of disinfectant and alcohol, but nothing calmed her rankled feelings. Her stomach hadn't stopped churning since the previous afternoon's debacle. Damn Gabriel Thornton! Just who did he think he was?

Well, *she* wasn't some simpleminded schoolgirl, easily intimidated by a mere kiss! Her thoughts balked at the word *mere*, then skittered away from the toe-curling memory of masterful lips and raw male power. Granted, he'd taken her completely off guard, but that's because she'd been under the impression that the days of Neanderthal men were over and that a Texas drawl bespoke some old standard of Southern chivalry.

Wrong on both accounts.

Well, she wouldn't make the mistake of underestimating him again. And there would be a next time. Someday, somewhere, Gabe Thornton would get his comeuppance, she guaranteed it. In the meantime, she still had to do her best for Gramps, and she was fresh out of ideas.

The bedside phone jangled, and she jumped to catch it on the first ring. Gramps murmured something indistinguishable and fitful, then subsided, snoring softly again.

"Sarah Ann, is that you?"

Suppressing a grimace of irritation, she tugged the phone cord to its length and stepped to the window to peer out between the slats. Her voice was low. "Hello, Douglas."

Douglas Ritchie's well-modulated words rumbled over the line. "Can you speak up? I can hardly hear you."

"Gramps is sleeping." Absently, she untucked her plain knit shirt from the waistband of her denim shorts and pulled her ponytail loose, getting more comfortable for the evening visiting hours still ahead of her.

"How is he today?"

"About the same." She combed tired fingers through the mass of her hair, sighing at the sensation. "Weak."

"And the doctors still don't have any answers? That's unacceptable. If I were you, I'd start thinking about malpractice—"

She stiffened. "Not now, Douglas, please."

"I'm sorry, sweetheart. That was thoughtless. You know I'd never do anything to upset you."

"Yes, I know."

That was the whole problem, Sarah Ann thought. How did you tell a nice guy and successful Realtor like Douglas Ritchie that you just weren't interested?

Gabe's blunt question "Don't you have a boyfriend...?" rang in her ears again, staining her cheeks with chagrin.

While she wouldn't exactly call herself experienced, she'd had several, thank you very much, including one serious beau she'd almost married before she'd dropped out of college to help Gramps. Her almost-fiancé had opted out at that point, unwilling to take on a wife with responsibilities.

After that disappointment she'd been much too busy to worry about her social life. It was hard to cultivate those kinds of friendships when you were up at dawn running a struggling tomato farm and orange groves, keeping up with the bookkeeping, taking up the slack in the warehouse, even doing some of the tractor driving, then falling into bed exhausted every night.

Lately, however, there was a difference of opinion on the boyfriend question, at least in Lostman's Island. But just because you'd been going out occasionally for the past year with the only guy who asked, and the whole town had begun to assume you were a couple, did that have to make it so?

Tall and bespectacled, Douglas was a soft-spoken teddy bear who'd been so solicitous during Gramps's illness Sarah

Ann would have felt like the most ungrateful wretch in the world to break things off. And she'd found it flattering to have a man pursue her, even though his conversation bored her to tears and his kisses were lackluster. But she felt guilty taking advantage of his good nature and had decided that the only honorable course of action was to gently, but firmly, decline any further invitations.

Unfortunately Douglas didn't seem to be getting the message. And to ask him to pretend to be her fiancé to ease Gramps's worries would only encourage him unnecessarily just when she most wanted to disentangle herself.

"Why don't you let me take you out for dinner tonight?" he asked. "I hear the Cotton Patch has great chicken-fried steak."

The thought of a greasy, crusty mass of beef in a plastic basket of fries held even less appeal than making conversation with Douglas. "Thanks, but I really can't."

"You're swamped taking care of the farm and staying at the hospital, too, aren't you? Sure, sweetheart, I understand." His words were full of kindness and concern and made Sarah Ann feel guiltier than ever.

"You try to do too much," he said. "One of these days you're going to have to let me help you out from under all that responsibility. I'll call you tomorrow."

"That's not nec—" The dial tone buzzed in her ear. Chewing her lip, she turned to hang up the receiver.

"You ought not to turn the boy down. He'll get discouraged."

Smiling into a pair of surprisingly bright blue eyes, Sarah Ann bent over the bed and squeezed her grandfather's hand. His deeply tanned skin was wrinkled from a lifetime of outdoor work, but his halo of wispy gray hair gave him a gnomish charm.

"Hey, there, sleepyhead. How was your nap?"

"Don't change the subject, girlie. That Douglas would marry you in a minute if you'd give him the least bit of encouragement."

She kept her voice light. "I'm not in love with Douglas."

"Pshaw." Harlan's face was drawn with fatigue, but his spirit was as cantankerous as ever. "What do young folks know about that? Time was when two people—"

"Did I tell you Charlie came by with the 'dozer bid?" Sarah Ann interrupted. "If we get those damaged orchards cleared, we can replant right away."

"Damn hurricanes. Always causing trouble," he grumbled, sidetracked for the moment. "What about the roof on the tractor shed?"

"That's next on the list." She mentally counted all the other things that needed doing, too. The thought of climbing a ladder and hammering tin filled her with dread, but she'd do what she had to do. She always did. Keeping her tone cheerful, she added, "Oh, and we got next season's contracts from the farmers co-op."

"Those orange-eating buzzards! Until some other outfit puts in a new processing plant and gives them some competition, they'll try to steal us blind."

"I can handle it, Gramps."

"No, dad-blame it, you can't!" In the blink of an eye, Harlan worked himself into a state, harping back over ground they'd covered time and again. "And I won't be around to tend to things for you."

"Don't say that, Gramps." She tried vainly to keep the distress out of her voice. "You're going to get well and come home very soon."

"Time to face facts, girlie." He wheezed painfully, and his gnarled, work-worn hands made restless circles across the white sheets. "Looks like I've run out of aces. Damnation, but I thought you'd be settled with a good man and a passel of babies by now. If you and Douglas—"

"Forget about him."

He slapped a shaky fist against the bed rail, his voice quivering with both anger and physical weakness. "If you aren't going to marry the boy, then I'm going to take him up on his offer."

"What offer?"

"To buy the whole place, lock, stock and barrel."

Shock widened her eyes. "What!"

Harlan nodded. "He said he'd be glad to help out, and that'll give you a nest egg. If you're set on being an old maid, the least I can do is leave you the money to go back to college and finish out that teacher's degree."

"I don't want that. And I can't believe you'd sacrifice everything we've built for this crazy notion!"

"Crazy, am I?" Mounting agitation mottled his pallid skin, and his chest heaved. "Pass me that there phone, and I'll show you what's what!"

The look on his face alarmed her, as did the racking cough that shook his wiry frame.

"That's all right, Gramps. Let's talk calmly about it, okay?" She tried to placate him with a smile and reached for the plastic pitcher and glass on the bedside table. "Here, have some water."

"Hand me the dad-blamed phone!" He shoved the water glass aside, slopping icy liquid down the front of Sarah Ann's shirt. "I'm gonna see you're taken care of one way or t'other."

"Gramps, please—"

He scrabbled for the receiver, swinging IV tubing and coughing harshly. Someone knocked on the door. Nearly frantic with concern now, Sarah Ann rushed to admit the nurse.

Her hands froze on the door handle, and her mouth dropped open. She took in cowboy boots, long jeanclad legs and a white T-shirt stretched over broad shoulders. A pair of aviator sunglasses were hooked to the crew neck.

"What do *you* want?"

Gabe Thornton's jaw worked at that hostile demand, but his manner was diffident, even deferential. "Miss Dempsey. I hate to bother you here, but if you could spare a moment, I'd like a word."

"About what?" Fingers clutching the edge of the door, she cast an anxious glance over her shoulder, unnerved by Gramps's continued hacking.

Gabe's tawny gaze touched her, focused briefly on the damp knit clinging to her bosom, then hastily moved on. "My partners and I are very interested in that frontage property."

Her teeth snapped together. "You've got your nerve. Go away."

"If you'll just hear me out—"

"Sarah . . ."

At Gramps's strangled call, she forgot Gabe and rushed back to the bedside. Her grandfather's pallor had turned a dull bluish tint. "Oh, my God—Gramps!"

Helplessness and fear paralyzed her, but then Gabe Thornton was beside her, taking in the situation, moving quickly, efficiently, lifting Harlan to a more upright position as easily as if he were a child and stuffing pillows behind his back.

"Take it easy, old-timer." Gabe's husky drawl was reassuringly matter-of-fact and held nothing of Sarah Ann's panic. Balancing Harlan with one brawny arm, he slapped the call button on the wall, spoke quietly at the nurse's buzz. "Respiratory distress. Get in here. *Now.*"

To Sarah Ann's infinite gratitude, the imperative in his tone had a pair of nurses bursting through the door within seconds. Gabe transferred the patient to their capable ministrations. Terrified, Sarah Ann watched them work in a flurry of IV injections, blood pressure cuffs and oxygen tubing. Gabe took her elbow and gently tugged her out of the way.

"He'll be all right," he murmured.

She couldn't answer and was only vaguely aware that she'd clenched a fist into Gabe's shirt and was holding on to that anchor for dear life. He humored her, allowing the liberty, placing an arm across her back so that she was half-supported against the bulk of his chest. She didn't question the arrangement, merely soaked up the strength that seemed to emanate from him along with the warm scent of his skin, a mixture of male musk and soap.

Although it seemed an eternity, within just a few minutes Harlan's breathing was less labored.

"That's a lot better, isn't it, Mr. Dempsey?" the head nurse asked cheerfully. Fifty and stout, Lillian Cannon was no-nonsense, performing her duties and directing her younger companion with absolute control and competency. Over the bed she caught Sarah Ann's eye and mouthed, "He's okay now."

Sarah Ann slumped with relief, bowing her head and resting it for the briefest of seconds against Gabe's chest. Her heart cried out with the sure foreknowledge of grief to come. "Okay" for now, she thought. But for how much longer?

She had the fleeting sensation of sympathetic fingers stroking her hair. Before she could decide if she was mistaken, embarrassment slammed into her. Cheeks heating, she tried to pull away, too chagrined to even look at Gabe. He let her retreat a bit, but only to guide her with a hand in the small of her back to her grandfather's bedside. Gramps watched them approach, his blue eyes tired over the clear plastic oxygen mask covering his nose.

"You rest now, Mr. Dempsey," Lillian said, patting his hand. Then, to Sarah Ann, "Do you know what brought this on?"

Guiltily, she swallowed hard and nodded. "A difference of opinion."

The head nurse gave her a stern look, the kind that said disturbing seriously ill patients in this manner was beneath contempt. "Dr. Stephens said we've got to avoid this kind of upset at any cost, you know that."

"Yes."

"As long as we understand each other. *At any cost.*"

Nodding, Lillian signaled her companion and they left. For all that he'd been a great help, Sarah Ann wished fervently Gabe would do the same. Instead, he stood behind her with his arms crossed over his broad chest, a slight frown puckering his brow. Ignoring him, she leaned over the bed rail, trying to make her smile both teasing and encouraging.

"Whew, that was something. But you always like to be the life of the party, don't you, Gramps?"

Harlan scowled, noticed Gabe then, and managed a croak. "Who—?"

"This is our new neighbor, Gabe Thornton," Sarah Ann said stiffly, remembering why Gabe was here.

The old man looked blank.

"We talked a while back about a piece of frontage property, Mr. Dempsey," Gabe explained.

At the mention of property, Harlan's regard snapped back to Sarah Ann. Behind the mask his words were muffled, but clear. "Call Douglas."

Dismay chilled her. Even after what he'd just been through, he still wouldn't give up. "We don't need him."

Agitation returning, he struggled to sit up. "Dad-blame it, girlie, I said do it!"

She knew with a certainty that he'd kill himself over this—right before her eyes, here, this minute—if she didn't do something. Something drastic. Something desperate. Something outrageous.

"I've been trying to tell you, Gramps. I've got wonderful news." Turning, Sarah Ann caught Gabe's hand. Laying it lovingly on the damp spot between her breasts, she beamed up into his stunned face. "Gabriel asked me to marry him—and I said yes!"

"You can't tell him the truth. Do you want to kill him outright?"

Floating on the evening twilight, Gabe's voice was savage. "No, it's *you* I'm liable to murder, lady! Get in."

Hauling Sarah Ann around by the arm, he reached for the driver's door of his army green Jeep. Balking, she tried to dig her heels into the sun-warmed asphalt of the hospital parking lot.

"Hold it, buster! I'm not going anywhere with you!"

"The way I see it, you got no choice." He thrust her into the vehicle, shoving her over into the passenger side as he slid under the wheel. She made a grab for the opposite door handle, but he dragged her back with a jerk. "Sit still."

"Listen, you—"

"Can it, sister. We're going to talk, that's all, and I want the shouting to take place out of earshot."

She quit struggling. "Oh."

He waited a moment more, then released her arm. "That's more like it."

Scooting into the corner as far away from him as she could, she sent him a resentful look. "I'm sick of your caveman tactics. You manhandle me again and you'll be walking funny."

Propping his forearm on the steering wheel, Gabe inspected her from her flowing mane to the slender but shapely turn of her ankles. Her legs weren't half-bad, actually, he thought, and she blushed at his perusal and tugged uncomfortably at the hem of her shorts. Enjoying her squirming, he blessed her with a sour smile.

"Big talk from a gal your size. Want to try best-two-out-of-three falls and see who wins?"

"That's right, resort to brute strength when all else fails," she said with a disdainful sniff. "It's no more than I'd expect from your type."

"Me? I've seen less ruthless behavior from a cobra! You want to tell me why the hell you told your grandpa that bald-faced lie?"

"You know why. You saw how he was," she muttered. Then her eyes flashed blue-violet in the dusky light. "And you're the biggest whiner I ever saw. I told you I'd give you the frontage property for doing this one little favor. What more do you want?"

Gabe rubbed his palms down his jaws and contemplated various forms of mayhem. "Not to be involved at all would be nice."

"Why don't you accept this gracefully?" She heaved a sigh at the glower he shot at her. "All right, I know I've taken advantage, but for a few hours of playacting, you get what you want as well as the satisfaction of sparing an old man needless suffering."

"Don't kid me that this is a selfless act. You're getting something out of it, too."

"I love my grandfather, not that you'd understand anything as simple as that!" she snapped. "You're just mad because you've been outmaneuvered by a female."

Gabe felt himself bristling. "Look, lady, I don't know you or your grandpa from Adam. What if I'm the kind of guy who can say the hell with you and him, too?"

She was silent for a long moment, then spoke slowly, her voice husky. "I guess I'm betting you aren't."

That took the wind out of his sails. "Oh, hell."

She spread her hands in appeal. "Please, Gabriel. I'm really desperate. You saw how happy the news made Gramps, how relieved he was. If I can give him that much before..."

She choked to a stop, pressing her knuckles to her lips. Gabe felt his anger slipping away, along with his resolve. Whatever he felt about this crazy scheme, it was clear she genuinely adored her grandfather. He felt a pang of envy. A woman who cared this deeply would be a prize to anyone she loved.

Rather desperately, he said, "But he wants to witness 'our' wedding. You heard him. Have the ceremony in his room, for God's sake!"

Sarah Ann licked her lips. "We could fake it."

Her words flabbergasted him, but it was the sight of her tongue darting over her lush mouth that made his belly tighten. Beset by the memory of her taste, he groaned silently and forced the feelings back.

No, he hadn't been with a woman in a while, and no, he was *not* going to let an unexpected and unwelcome flash of sexual hunger further complicate this already muddled situation. Hell, he didn't even like this little conniver!

"You've got to be kidding," he croaked.

"It wouldn't be that hard. We just need someone to play justice of the peace. It won't be elaborate. Five minutes is all. Perhaps one of your friends—?"

"God, no!" The thought of explaining all this to Mike and Rafe made him shudder. Talk about looking like a fool!

"Then I'll find someone," she said. "There are always people looking to make a few bucks. And I'll arrange everything else—the ceremony, the rings, the deed of transfer on the land—everything. So...will you do it?"

Feeling boxed in, Gabe rubbed his pounding temple. "I must be as crazy as you are."

She leaned forward, hopeful. "Then you will?"

Gabe grimaced. In service to his country, he'd been a weapon, and an effective one, but he drew the line at killing old men with words—even truthful ones. So he would mangle his self-respect for a few hours to humor this eccentric female and earn a chunk of land for his trouble. At least his partners would be happy.

"Thanks to you, I don't have much choice, do I?"

Her breath left her in a little relieved puff. Reaching out, she placed a tentative hand on his shoulder, a peace offering that made his skin burn through the thin knit of his shirt.

"Thank you." In the gathering darkness, her whisper was breathless with gratitude. "You won't regret it. It won't take much time, and after it's all over, I'll never bother you again."

With a prick of foreboding, Gabe wondered if that was a promise or a threat.

Three days later Sarah Ann walked toward Gramps's hospital room, her seldom-worn dress pumps clicking against the polished tiles like an executioner's drumroll.

Though the corridor was chilly with air-conditioning, she was perspiring beneath her off-white linen sheath, a condition that could only be attributed to a bad case of prenuptial jitters.

Not that what she was about to do with Gabriel Thornton was in any sense real, of course, she told herself sternly. But for Gramps's sake, even going through the motions had to look genuine.

At six o'clock she would meet Gabe and they would mouth words before a man she'd hired to play the part of justice of the peace. The cousin of a friend of one of her farm hands, he'd assured her he understood her need for discretion, that he'd meet them at the hospital room primed for his role, and that the ceremony would be "a piece of cake."

That piece of out-and-out dishonesty weighed heavily enough, but the preparations for the actual ceremony itself, deciding what to wear—the plain dress, her mother's pearls—and how to fix her hair—a French twist to control her waves—had produced an artificial excitement that tied her into nervous knots. She prayed that for the few minutes it took, she could play the part of happy, blushing bride without throwing up.

As she turned a corner, Sarah Ann's steps faltered at the sight of the tall figure leaning against the windowsill opposite Gramps's doorway. Swallowing, she realized Gabe had done his breathtaking best to look the part, too. In dark suit and conservative tie, he was a solemn stranger, enigmatic and unapproachable, somewhat frightening, totally fascinating.

Who was he, really? she wondered. It was a bit disheartening to realize that it didn't matter, for by her own choice his role in her life could be only temporary.

Gabe looked up at the sound of her steps, then straightened to his full height, his eyes piercing her, golden as an eagle's.

"Hi."

She tried to smile. "Hello."

He inspected her—the simple dress, her trembling hands, the upswept hairdo—and something hungry flared in his expression, then was gone. "You look nice."

"Thanks. So do you."

She knew her words were stiff, inane, and she closed her eyes briefly, praying for lucidity and composure. She had to get through this—after all, it was her idea! *It's just business,* she recited like a mantra.

Reaching into her small clutch purse, she passed him a folded document. "Your deed. Everything's filed at the courthouse."

He shoved the paper inside his jacket without looking at it. "Thank you."

"And here are the rings. I had to guess at the size." With a tremulous laugh, she passed him a small box, and he shoved it into a pants pocket. "Lord, this is awkward, isn't it?"

"Deception always is, Sarah."

Stricken, she didn't know what to say. Frowning, Gabe raised his hand and touched her face, running a thumb under her jawbone, gently fingering the pearl stud in her ear.

"I forget you're a novice at this kind of thing," he muttered. "Don't worry, sweetheart, I'm an old hand at it. I'll guide you through."

The warmth of his skin stroking hers made her shiver. "Is that supposed to reassure me?"

A slow grin curled his mouth. "It should."

"I'll try to remember."

"In the meantime..." Turning to the windowsill, he picked up a bundle, removed a layer of tissue and offered her a ribbon-wrapped bouquet of red roses. "Maybe you should hold on to these."

Mystified, touched beyond words, she took the flowers, marveling at their velvety texture and inhaling their sweetness. "Oh, Gabe, they're exquisite."

"Just doing my part to keep up appearances."

Like a dash of cold water, that jolted her from her haze. *It's just business.* "Well, thank you. You shouldn't have gone to the trouble."

"Beulah cut them."

Sarah Ann sucked in a breath. "You told her? About this?"

"What do you think I am—crazy? No, don't answer that." He shook his head, his brow wrinkling as if pondering a riddle. "But she left them on the table, and they looked right, so here they are. How she knew...sometimes I think she's a witch."

"At any rate, it's a nice touch. You should have one, too." She plucked a bud and stuck it in his lapel. "They're really quite lovely."

"Yeah." He searched her face for a long moment, then tucked her hand into the crook of his arm. "Ready to get this over with?"

Drawing a breath for courage, she nodded. "Yes."

Gabe pushed open the door and ushered her inside.

"There they are," Gramps said in a hearty voice. "About time!"

Sarah Ann blinked, taken aback by the unexpected sea of smiling faces that greeted them. Gramps sat propped upright in his bed, clean-shaven and looking dapper and more cheerful than he had in weeks. Beside him stood his oldest friend, retired Judge Henry Holt, stout and graying, but still vigorous at seventy-five. A fresh-faced young man wearing a rather shiny suit and holding a Bible stood before a makeshift bower of flowers and greenery, apparently the work of Lillian, the head nurse, and her staff, who waited to one side, white uniformed and dewy-eyed with expectation.

"My goodness." Sarah Ann's voice was faint. Beside her, Gabe breathed an expletive.

Lillian bustled up to them, all goodwill. "Now, don't be upset with our little surprise, Sarah Ann. When Harlan told us your plans, we just couldn't help getting into the spirit of things. I hope you don't mind."

"Oh, no, of course not."

"I know how busy you've been, and of course, all the details, the blood tests—"

"Blood tests?" Sarah Ann echoed, shooting a wide-eyed glance at Gabe.

"Don't tell me you forgot?" Lillian asked. Reading Sarah Ann's dismay and totally misinterpreting it, she took charge. "Well, we can take care of that right now! Charlotte, hand me that tray."

Before they had a chance to protest, Lillian pricked their fingers, prepared slides and sent the tray off to the lab.

"There, all done. A whirlwind courtship, wasn't it? It's so romantic," the nurse said with a sigh. She patted Gabe's arm. "Congratulations, young man. You're getting a mighty fine gal."

Gabe cleared his throat. "Thank you, ma'am."

"Come here, girlie, and give your old Gramps a hug," Harlan ordered from the bed. Sarah Ann obliged. When she released him, Harlan offered his hand to Gabe, shook it soundly. "I want to welcome you to the family, son. You're both making me a mighty happy man today."

Gabe cleared his throat again. "Thank you, sir."

"I'm glad you're happy, Gramps." Tears prickled behind Sarah Ann's lids.

"Now, none of that," he chided, then turned to his old friend. "Tell her, Henry. It's a happy time."

"Good gracious, yes!" the judge agreed. "And this is your intended?"

He pumped Gabe's hand, beaming. "Harlan asked me to be a witness. Flat tickled me, I don't mind telling you. Got all the necessary paperwork right here." He patted his jacket pocket. "I knew you wouldn't mind, so I've taken care of everything. I still have some pull down at the courthouse. Got you one of their gold-embossed licenses. Made it real special."

"Ah, Sarah and I appreciate it," Gabe said, his words strangled.

"Are we ready to get started?" the young man with the Bible asked hopefully.

"Absolutely!" Gabe took Sarah Ann's arm and positioned them in front of the bower, evoking a titter of indulgent laughter from the witnesses at his apparent eagerness.

Only Sarah Ann knew that it was really his desperation to have this charade behind them, and it matched her own. She'd had no idea it would be so hard! At least her counterfeit justice of the peace was ready to do the job he'd been paid for. She caught his eye, trying to convey silent messages: Get on with it! Make it look good! Hurry!

All she got was a puzzled look in return, but then he started reading with all due solemnity and restored her confidence. "Dearly Beloved . . ."

It was the work of barely five minutes, the recitation of names, the exchange of rings and vows. Sarah Ann's fingers were icy; Gabe's replies as wooden as her own. *Fraud,* her guilty conscience whispered. *Liar.* But one look at

Gramps's face, and she knew she would do it all again, a hundred times over if necessary.

The young man closed his Bible, smiling cordially at the couple in front of him. "Now, by the power vested in me by the state of Florida—"

The door burst open, spilling bodies and boisterous commotion into the already-overcrowded room.

"Where's the wedding?" roared a swarthy man with oiled-down hair and a polyester suit. His eyes lit up in triumph at the sight of flowers and guests, but his voice was slurred. "Oh, ho, fellows! This has gotta be the place! Had a hell of a time finding it, though, didn't we? Why don't they have more signs? We ain't brain surgeons."

His scruffy companions nodded, laughed uproariously at this apparent witticism and leered at the group of nurses. Revolted, Sarah Ann took an involuntary step backward, grateful to have Gabe's protecting arm at her waist.

"Here now, what's the meaning of this?" Judge Holt demanded. "Good God, man, you're drunk!"

"I ain't," the intruder replied indignantly. He lifted a beer bottle and grinned. "Just celebrating the festivities ahead of time. Carrot-headed fellow down at the Whistling Pirate kept buying rounds, ain't that right, boys?"

"A swell guy," one of his friends agreed. "Big, too. Drink a keg of beer all by himself."

"Well, we sure gave him some help." Taking a final swallow, the leader tossed the empty bottle in a nearby wastebasket, rubbed his hands, and looked around expectantly. "Okay, let's get this show on the road!"

"Mister," Gabe growled, "I'm going to have to ask you to leave."

"Wait a minute! I been hired to do a job, and by gum, I'm gonna do it! Which one of you is the Dempsey gal? You want a justice of the peace or not?"

"Justice of the—" Horror stole Sarah Ann's breath, clogged her throat. "You?"

Belligerent now, the man scowled. "You hired mc, didn't you? Paid good money for this part. Just 'cause a man's a little late..."

She swung to the man holding the Bible. "Then who's this?"

"Why, Reverend Cullen, girlie," Harlan said. "The new hospital chaplain."

Sarah Ann's knees buckled. Gabe caught her, steadying her until she found her feet again. Their eyes met. Realization dawned. An ordained clergyman. Blood tests. The judge's license.

She saw the wrath building in Gabe's expression, saw the house of cards she'd been trying to build for Gramps tumble and fall. Panic consumed her, made her voice a thin wail. "Oh, my God."

"We're churchgoing folks," Harlan continued. "I couldn't have my granddaughter married by a civil servant."

"Certainly not!" Lillian snapped, recovering her authority. "And this one's a pure disgrace to his calling! You men, out!" Like a drill sergeant, she herded the protesting intruders outside, slammed the door behind them and restored order. "Go ahead, Reverend."

Nonplussed, Reverend Cullen fumbled with the Bible. "Uh, ahem. Where were we? Oh, yes."

Trapped within the circle of Gabe's arms, Sarah Ann trembled uncontrollably as the clergyman blessed them with a benign smile.

"I now pronounce you husband and wife. You may kiss your bride."

Three

Husband.
  Wife.
  Gabe stared down into Sarah Ann's pansy-colored eyes and saw hysteria blossoming. From long experience in the face of unmitigated disaster, he knew the only alternative was damage control.

  So he took the preacher's suggestion and kissed her.

  To keep her quiet, he told himself, molding his mouth against hers.

  To keep up appearances for the old man's sake, he assured himself, holding her still with a hand to the back of her head.

  To keep the situation from blowing wide open in front of all these witnesses, he said inwardly, deepening the kiss.

  And to see if she still tasted of spice and promise.
  She did.

With a groan of impatience, Gabe tightened his hold and brought them both closer to the edge of forgetfulness. She'd been quaking in his arms, but now she melted against him, her subtle curves complementing his hard angles. Growing pliant, quiescent, she warmed to the heat of his lips, opening for him. She looped her arms around his neck, and the rich perfume of her bouquet filled his head, made him dizzy with desire.

Which wasn't his original intention at all.

Coming to his senses, Gabe broke off the kiss, pushing Sarah Ann's face into the crook of his shoulder, his breathing gusty, his heart pounding. Holding her protectively, his mouth against the delicate shell of her ear, he whispered to her, the picture of the tender and devoted lover, but his low tone was harsh with anger directed at himself and his lack of control.

"For God's sake, get a grip." He felt her jerk, but easily contained her involuntary movement. "Don't panic."

Muffled against his shirt collar, her words were barely audible. "Let me go, you bastard."

"Listen to me, damn you." His fingers tightened in her hair. "Everyone's watching. Get hold of yourself. Put on a smile and look like you're in love, or you'll blow everything."

He sensed her surprise. What had she expected? he thought. That he'd call the whole thing off because of this cosmic blunder, revealing them both as liars and fools or worse? Not bloody damn likely!

He waited until the subtle tension in her limbs indicated a semblance of composure, however brittle, then gingerly released her.

Sliding her arms from around his neck, she gave him a smile that never reached her eyes and murmured, "I hate and despise you."

His expression was equally affectionate, equally false. "The feeling's mutual, sweetheart."

"Oh, my goodness, I think I'm going to cry!" Lillian bustled forward to envelop Sarah Ann in a warm hug. "Every happiness, my dear."

They were immediately surrounded by a bevy of well-wishers. Gabe did his best to accept the congratulations heaped upon him with something approaching equanimity. He was hard-pressed to know what else to do, except follow the old military tactics of falling back to regroup in the face of a total rout.

He nearly lost his poise when Judge Holt pressed a pen into his hands to sign the fancy license. Short of confessing to their false intentions on the spot, there was no alternative. With a look that dared her to do less, he passed the pen to Sarah Ann. She swallowed hard, then scratched her name on the line beside his.

It was a bizarre way to acquire a wife, and it produced a peculiar tickling in the back of his mind, as if demons or angels performed a frenzied tarantella on his synapses at his expense. Gabe shrugged to himself. Well, there had to be legal remedies to this situation, strange as it was, and since Reverend Cullen and the nurses were already taking their leave, he'd find a way to extricate himself from this little party real soon, too. Until then, his best bet was to follow his own advice and refuse to panic.

"Oh, no, Gramps, we really couldn't." Sarah Ann stood at the hospital bed with Judge Holt. The thin edge of alarm in her voice snagged Gabe's attention.

"Nonsense, girlie," the old man said. "I insist. I know you. You'll think you have to sit here with me or some such foolishness."

"I really shouldn't leave you—"

"I'm tired out from the excitement. I'll just go on to sleep, whether you're here or not. What do I want with more company?" He gestured to Gabe. "You talk some sense into her, son."

"Yes, sir. As soon as you tell me how it's done."

Harlan chuckled. "He's got your number already, girlie."

Distress tugged at Sarah Ann's mouth—her well-kissed mouth, Gabe noted, then forcibly curtailed that wayward thought.

"We . . . we planned to spend a quiet evening," she said, shooting Gabe a frantic glance. "At . . . at home."

Harlan shook his head, emphatic. "I won't hear of it. Besides, it's all arranged, isn't it, Henry?"

"Yes, indeed." The judge beamed his pleasure. "I'm official chauffeur."

"To where?" Gabe asked carefully.

"The honeymoon suite at the best hotel in Lostman's Island." Harlan smiled in satisfaction. "It's my wedding gift to you two kids."

"Good God, woman, stop looking at me like that—I'm not going to pounce on you!"

Heart in her throat, Sarah Ann watched Gabe prowl the perimeter of their luxurious suite like a caged tiger. Taking his assignment seriously, Judge Holt had ushered them inside moments before, wishing them a good night's rest with a twinkle in his eye.

But considering the way Gabe had kissed her into putty earlier, and worse, the shameless way she'd responded, Sarah Ann wasn't reassured by Gabe's growled declaration. He was livid, and he had a right to be.

Looking away from Gabe's intimidating scowl, she let her gaze wander the room. Gramps had really gone all out.

The Victoria, a turn-of-the-century bed and breakfast establishment, was a haven of antiques, plush fabrics and fresh flowers. A four-poster bed draped with netting sat on a pastel oriental rug. A magnum of champagne cooled in a sterling ice bucket. A pair of terry cloth robes hung in the bath beside the huge claw-footed tub, and the judge had even supplied overnight kits for them both. Soft lighting and softer music added to the ambiance.

It was all perfectly romantic, a setting ripe for seduction, and under the circumstances it scared the bejesus out of her.

"I'm sorry," she said, gulping. Knees wobbling, she sank down onto the edge of an apricot velvet chaise and pressed trembling fingers to her lips. "I don't know how this happened."

"Beats the hell out of me, too." He flicked his collar button with his thumb, then stripped off his jacket and tie and flung them on the foot of the bed.

To Sarah Ann, it was a gesture of alarming intimacy. Her breath caught on a little desperate gasp. "We'll get an annulment."

His scowl grew darker. "That goes without saying, sweetheart. I never bargained for the real thing, and, as I recall, no one was even supposed to know about that so-called wedding."

"I had no idea Gramps would tell anyone. And it was only a few people." She shrugged helplessly. "It'll blow over."

His look was ominous. "It had better."

There was a discreet knock. Their glances met, then Gabe went to the door. A young, smiling waiter pushed a cart loaded with covered dishes, sparkling crystal and a single red rose in a bud vase into the room.

"Your grandpa knows how to pull out all the stops," Gabe said sourly. He reached into his pants pocket and passed the waiter some bills. "Thanks, buddy."

The young man nodded, tried to suppress a smirk, but couldn't. "Enjoy yourself, mister."

As the door closed, Sarah Ann's face flamed, and she surged to her feet. "Look, there's no reason we have to stay here—"

"Hell, the way my luck is running, Harlan's probably got the place under surveillance!"

"That's ridiculous." Her breathing accelerated. "And if that's your attitude, you can just go to hell."

His eyes narrowed, molten with growing ire. "You're doing it again."

She blinked, startled. "Doing what?"

"Looking as though I'm about to eat you alive." Gabe caught her arms, crowding her so that the backs of her knees pressed against the chaise. "Though it's no more than you deserve."

A bolt passed through her middle, making her shiver, and she pressed a restraining hand against his shirtfront. "Leave me alone."

"What's the matter?" he mocked softly. "Never considered there might be a price to pay for all your lies? What if I decided to take my payment for this mess you've gotten me into out of your pretty hide? Hell, it would even be legal!"

"And risk your annulment?" Defiant, scornful, she glared at him. "That would make a lot of sense! Go right ahead."

"Don't push me, lady."

She wilted under his uncompromising stare. "Gabe, believe me, I never expected anything like this to happen! We'll get it all untangled, I promise."

"So far, your promises haven't been worth much." His hands tightened on her. "And it doesn't help my frame of mind for you to think I'm Satan incarnate."

"I never said—"

"Because if I were, I'd be doing something like this." Bending, he nuzzled the curve of her neck, riffling chill bumps to every extremity.

She gasped. "Stop that!"

"Or maybe this."

He kissed the inside angle of her elbow, then let his lips glide down her forearm to her hand. His teeth nipped the fleshy pad at the base of her thumb, shocking her into retaliation. But he was faster, catching the hand she raised to strike him and twisting it behind her back, forcing their lower bodies into intimate contact.

"You're full of surprises," he murmured, his grin wolfish.

"And you're vile!"

"Thank you, ma'am, I try." His tawny eyes glinted, and he caught her chin, inspecting her face with such intensity her mouth went dry.

Caught, pressed hip to hip, Sarah Ann stared up at him. She was so close she could see the haze of golden stubble that shadowed his lean jaw and smell the musky scent of his skin, warm and male and unsettling. For all his Texas gentility, she knew that an outlaw lurked inside him, wild and untamed. Her voice was strange, husky to her own ears. "What are you doing?"

"Satisfying my curiosity." Digging fingers into her hair, he plucked pins free until her curls tumbled to her shoulders. "You tease a man, make him wonder—"

"I didn't!"

"—sometimes things can get out of hand." He brushed his lips over her ear, down the curve of her cheekbone, then let them hover over her mouth, tantalizing and terrifying. She could barely breathe.

"Why are you doing this?" she whispered, mesmerized.

He flicked a finger over her lower lip. "Dumb question, Sarah Ann."

"To punish me," she accused. "You have a mean streak in you, Gabriel Thornton."

"It's best you remember that."

She shivered. "You are a devil."

"Sweetheart, a saint would be hard-pressed to resist an armful of temptation like you." His lips twisted. "So I guess this makes me one of the heavenly hosts."

He released her and stepped back, leaving her gasping for air and wondering what he meant. Temptation? Her? Since when? It was just another cruelty to taunt her lack of sophistication and desirability in such a despicable fashion!

Sauntering to the food cart, he raised one sandy eyebrow in inquiry. "Dinner, ma'am?"

Sarah Ann sank back down on the chaise with a thump of disbelief. He'd had the audacity to insult her, to turn her inside out, to make her furious and melting and miserable all at the same time, and now he wanted to talk about food? The man was unbelievable!

"How can you eat?" she demanded.

"In my former line of work, I learned to always take whatever advantage there was of a situation. And I'm hungry."

He rummaged among the dishes, giving a grunt of satisfaction at the prime rib and potatoes, salad and strawberries. Deftly, he uncorked the champagne, poured two glasses, then brought one to Sarah Ann.

"Here, you look as though you could use this."

"Small wonder, thanks to you." Feeling mutinous and resentful, she drained the glass, gasping a little as the effervescence filled her sinuses.

"Hey, watch it! That stuff will get to you in a hurry."

"I'm a big girl, used to taking care of myself, okay?" She stuck the glass out for more. "Shut up and pour."

Shrugging, he refilled her glass. "Suit yourself."

He placed one dinner plate on the end table beside the chaise, then took his own dish and perched on the edge of the bed to eat.

Sarah Ann sipped champagne along with her defiance. Gabe endured her stony silence and harder looks until his plate was nearly empty, then, with an exasperated exhalation, suddenly stood and shoved the dish back onto the cart.

"You can forget this cold shoulder treatment. It's not going to accomplish anything."

The wine was beginning to have a calming effect, but Sarah Ann kept her tone cool, lofty. "I don't know what you mean."

"Look, I apologize, okay?" He shoved his fists into his pants pockets. "I was out of line before. My temper seldom gets the best of me, but something about you ..."

"I'm scarcely responsible for your bad manners," she snapped.

"That's not what I meant." He pushed aggravated fingers through his sun-streaked hair, found a tender spot and rubbed his scalp as if to soothe it and his own frustration. "Lord, you can twist a man's words into pure trouble."

"You do quite a capable job of that on your own."

"Normally, I'm the most even tempered of men."

Maybe it was the wine, maybe it was a sense that a full belly and a little time had mellowed his dangerous mood, but Gabe's assertion struck her as funny. She laughed out loud. "You couldn't prove it by me!"

His expression was vaguely sheepish. "I guess not." Then he cocked his head, inspecting her. "You should do that more often."

"What?" She looked into the bottom of her goblet and was surprised to find it empty again. "Guzzle champagne?"

"No, laugh like that. It shows off how pretty you are."

A flush that had nothing to do with the wine she'd consumed flooded Sarah Ann's cheeks. She set her glass down with too much force, making the crystal ping quietly, and avoided Gabe's eyes. "I wish you wouldn't say things like that."

"Why not?"

"Despite everything—" she waved a vague hand "—this is a business relationship."

"But why does it make you uncomfortable?"

"Because I know it isn't true."

His jaw went slack with disbelief. "Lady, you should look in the mirror more often."

"I don't really think this is appropriate—"

Now it was his turn to laugh. "Oh, no? Somehow, for two people who just got *married,* it might be."

"Yes, and that's just the problem, isn't it?" She rubbed her temple, brushing away wayward curls and the beginnings of a headache. "We've got to figure some way out of this!"

Throwing himself down on the edge of the bed, Gabe began to roll up his cuffs. "Oh, hell, relax. There's nothing we can do about it now, so let's not sweat the small stuff."

"What do you mean?"

A rueful grimace flattened his mouth. "Despite my bellowing like a stuck calf, nothing's really changed, except for pursuing a legal annulment, and that shouldn't present much difficulty."

She looked hopeful. "You think not?"

"It'll take some time, that's all. I'll find out. In the meantime, we'll just keep a very low profile. After all, this is nobody's business but ours, and you've got to concentrate on your grandfather. Later—" he shrugged, and for an instant his eyes were bleak "—well, marriages fall apart for different reasons. No one will think much of it, if they even notice at all."

"Yes." She nodded, feeling relieved, then bit her lip. "Gabe?"

"Yeah?"

"Will you still visit Gramps with me a time or two, just so he won't worry?"

Gabe frowned, but nodded. "It was part of the bargain."

"Tomorrow? He'll expect it."

"I've got a morning charter, but I could pick you up when I get back."

"Thank you. It means a lot."

Uncomfortable with her gratitude, he nodded at her forgotten plate. "You should eat something."

The champagne and his sudden kindness made her fuzzyheaded. "Perhaps you're right."

She plucked a strawberry from the plate and nibbled it, watching Gabe rearrange the bed's rose-patterned pillows and lace-edged bolsters. Finally, he settled back against the headboard and reached for the television remote control, looking incongruously and heart-stoppingly large and masculine among all the feminine frills.

"Maybe we can catch some news," he muttered, turning on the set located across from the foot of the bed.

It was something so normal, an action so male that Sarah Ann smiled. "I must say that after your initial—er, annoyance, you're taking this better than I'd hoped."

"Honey, I've seen worse." His gaze never left the flickering TV screen, but his lean features hardened. "Been worse. Done worse. A lot worse."

She couldn't constrain her curiosity. "Like what?"

His gaze went faraway, but his laugh was self-deprecating. "Believe me, you'd rather not know."

That gave her a tiny chill. "Why not?"

He looked at her then, his eyes flaring golden in the soft light. "Because then you'd know you've married a monster."

She caught her breath, and the lingering sweetness of the strawberry turned bitter in her mouth. A sitcom chirped in the background. "Are you trying to frighten me again?"

"Now, ma'am, would I do that?" he drawled.

Somehow, his insouciance didn't ring true. With an instinct as old as time, Sarah Ann sensed the wounds beneath the strength, understood the price he'd paid for being a lone wolf all his life. There were barriers there, walls only the most brave, or the most foolhardy, would attempt to breach.

"What happened?" she asked softly.

"I got out." He laughed again. "With my life, if not my sanity, as this situation clearly proves."

She made a little sound of distress. "How many times do you want me to apologize?"

A lazy smile curled his lips. "That all depends."

Trepidation squeezed her heart. "On what?"

Scowling at her sudden change of expression, he cursed under his breath. "There's that damn 'fawn caught in the headlights' look of yours again! You are too damned easy to terrorize, you know that?''

"You're pretty scary sometimes, Gabriel."

He scrubbed his jaw with his palm, perplexed and sty-mied by her honesty. "Look, let's just agree that we've had some monumental bad luck and cry peace for the dura-tion, okay?''

She slumped in relief. "All right."

"Good. So you eat your dinner, we'll watch some TV, and I'll figure a way to get us both out of this joint at some point tonight without giving the management a coronary.'' His tone was surly, daring her to disagree. "That suit you?''

"Fine." She couldn't help a faint edge of sarcasm. "Thank you for being so understanding.''

His jaw hardened, but all he said was, "Fine," then surfed through the channels as if it were the most fascinat-ing pastime ever invented.

With shaking fingers, Sarah Ann reached for the cham-pagne bottle and poured herself another glass, pointedly ignoring Gabe's raised eyebrow. It seemed a shame to let it go to waste. After all, she thought with a sense of renewed defiance, it was her honeymoon night—perhaps the only one she might ever have—and Gramps had gone to a lot of expense and trouble to make it memorable.

Not that she was likely to forget anything about this hu-miliating experience. The disturbing man lounging on the bed in his shirtsleeves had seen to that! But it could have been worse. She raised her glass in a silent toast, congrat-ulating herself. Gramps was happy, she and Gabe would get the annulment in due course, and she'd emerged relatively unscathed from the whole experience.

But down deep, in a place she refused to probe too closely, Sarah Ann knew the champagne she sipped was flat and that her relief felt shamefully like disappointment.

* * *

The Dempsey spread was disappointing, but then that's the way Gabe's whole day had gone, so he wasn't surprised.

Since the moment he'd delivered Sarah Ann to her truck in the hospital parking lot at dawn, mechanical troubles, demanding passengers and threatening weather had given him one headache after another. He'd left the tiny local airport, where he leased hangar space, with a great sense of relief, even though he wasn't at all looking forward to the promised visit to Harlan's bedside this afternoon.

Now a purple line of thunderheads gathered in the west over the Gulf as he drove up the shell-paved lane toward the white frame Dempsey house. He noticed withered tomato fields being plowed under for the end of the season by a single rusty tractor. The vegetable sheds stood empty and forlorn. Most disturbing of all were the dead gnarled trunks in the orange groves damaged by the previous fall's hurricanes.

No wonder Harlan had been beside himself with worry about Sarah Ann's future. The Dempseys were weathering a storm, all right, but from what could be seen, Gabe wondered how long they could hold out.

Parking his Jeep, Gabe inspected the house, a hipped-roof structure wrapped with screened porches and shaded by wind-stunted live oaks. Multicolored caladiums filled the front flower beds, but the paint was peeling and the roof sported odd blocks of shingles, where it had been patched with whatever had been at hand. Behind the house itself sat several barns and equipment sheds in which he could see machinery in a variety of conditions, from operable implements to mere decaying hulks.

Gabe climbed from his Jeep, a sense of déjà vu filling him. Despite the differences in crops, there was a feel about the Dempsey farm that reminded him of the Texas cattle ranch where he'd grown up. Shabby, struggling, there was always work to be done on a place like this, but the care evidenced by the tidy yard and well-repaired roof showed an undaunted spirit, a loving people who cared deeply about the land and about building something lasting.

Gabe's boots thumped on the wooden porch steps, and he paused to remove his sunglasses, letting his gaze roam, assessing the property, seeing beyond the shabbiness to the potential underneath. It was hard for a man like him to admit he missed his home, to feel such a pull of nostalgia and longing for the simplicity of childhood and hard work and a loving family...to admit that looking over the Dempsey place gave him a pang of pure envy.

Gabe shook his head. There was too much water under that bridge. Wasn't it Thomas Wolfe who'd said that you can never go home again? Besides, he had plenty on his plate with Angel's Landing and his charter service, and he'd put enough blisters on his hands growing up to swear never to find himself tied down to that kind of life again. It was what had driven him into the service in the first place. He decided it was his awful day that was making him so maudlin.

Or maybe it was one hell of a honeymoon night.

The air was sultry, thick, and a film of sweat dampened his skin. Grimacing, Gabe blotted his forehead against the sleeve of his grease-stained T-shirt. Heck, a man had a right to feel a bit restless, and maybe more than a little crazed, after watching the woman who was now legally his wife grow rumpled and drowsy on a velvet couch the color of apricots—all the while knowing that he couldn't touch her.

Even now, the memory made his mouth go dry. It was the age-old temptation of forbidden fruit, not that he was attracted to the strange little cat, he told himself firmly, even if her mouth was honey and spice and her slender curves fit his hands perfectly. She'd fallen asleep with her palm pressed beneath her cheek, as trusting as a child even after all that had passed between them, and somehow he'd found that most arousing of all. But he was accustomed to self-discipline, accustomed to disappointment, and the last thing he needed in his life was a wife.

Not that he was much of a catch himself, Gabe admitted with a sour touch of self-deprecating humor. He'd tried to make a go of it once, but his relationship with Andrea during their all-too-brief marriage had proven to him he wasn't good husband material. Too much of a loner, too dedicated to the job, the military, his buddies, everyone but her, she'd told him. A man who gave nothing of himself even when he was around, and he wasn't around much. Finally she'd found someone who was, and she'd left Gabe. The rejection hurt, but secretly he'd been relieved.

No, he just wasn't cut out for relationships, so it was a damned good thing this present marriage was just make-believe, simply an illusion of smoke and mirrors. And the sooner he removed himself from the near occasion of sin and temptation in the person of one Sarah Ann Dempsey by completing their bargain, obtaining the annulment and getting the hell out of her life, the better for all concerned.

Raising his fist, Gabe pounded on the screen door. No one answered. He tried again, calling Sarah Ann's name. No reply. Frowning, he pulled open the door, crossed the porch, then peeked inside the house. The homey front room was deserted, and no sounds came from the rear of the house.

He went back to the steps. Sarah Ann's absence was as disturbing as the thunder rumbling in the distance. Had something happened?

He stepped out into the yard, then made his way around back toward the sheds. Maybe she'd gotten tied up with some chore. Perhaps she'd lost track of time. Maybe she was in trouble. Perhaps she was lying hurt somewhere—

Suddenly the sound of hammering sliced through Gabe's churning thoughts. Following the noise, he strode around behind a dilapidated, tin-roofed shed, with two beat-up tractors and other miscellaneous equipment parked inside, to find a metal ladder propped against the eaves. Over his head the banging continued unabated. A flicker of lightning slashed through a lavender thunderhead just as a slight female figure lifted her hammer for another blow.

Lightning. Tin roof. Metal ladder. Steel hammerhead. The implications caught Gabe like a blow to the stomach. He went ballistic.

"What the *hell* do you think you're doing?"

Sarah Ann jerked at Gabe's roar, pivoting on her hands and knees to peer down at him. Her hair fell free from her ponytail; her face was pasty. The jeans and stretched-out T-shirt she wore were drenched in sweat and clung to her body. "You're here already?"

"Lady, get your butt down from there. *Now!*"

She gave him a puzzled look. "But I'm nearly finished—"

Gabe ground his teeth and yelled up at her. "You're going to be *dead* if you're not careful. Now move!"

Her mouth tightened in the mulish manner he was fast becoming familiar with. "Look, I don't take orders from you, *Captain,* so get that straight—"

"That tears it!" He stepped onto the first rung of the ladder. "You're coming down now if I have to drag you down by the scruff of your damned stubborn neck!"

The fierceness in his expression must have convinced her he meant business. "Okay, maybe you're right," she said hastily. "I'm coming. Hold your horses."

She scrambled to the top of the ladder, and Gabe got a bird's-eye view of a shapely female posterior as she backed carefully down. He grabbed her about the waist before she was halfway, swinging her to the ground, then giving her a shake that made her head snap back.

"What's the matter with you?" he shouted. "Are you out of your mind?"

"Stop yelling at me!" Her voice wobbled, and she swayed beneath Gabe's grasp. "You have no right—"

"Tell that to the judge, Mrs. Thornton," he snapped. "And if you think I'm going to let you kill yourself, simply because you're too damned stupid to come in out of a storm— What's the matter?"

"Let me go." She pushed at her hair with a shaky hand, her breathing too fast and shallow. "I don't feel well."

"You're green around the gills, all right. Too much champagne?" he asked nastily.

"You can take a flying leap—ohh." She staggered and would have fallen if Gabe hadn't scooped her up against his chest. She protested, her voice faint. "Put me down."

He was already heading back toward the house, impatience in his expression, exasperation in his stride. "Don't be any dumber than you have to be, okay?"

"I'm all right," she wailed against his shoulder.

"The hell you are. You're dealing with the champagne from last night and the beginnings of heat prostration."

Kicking open the door, Gabe carried her inside, passing the kitchen, then heading down the hall until he found the antiquated white-tiled bath. Setting her to her feet, he supported her with one arm while he turned the shower on full blast, then reached for the sodden hem of her shirt.

She gasped, her violet eyes wide with alarm. "What do you think you're doing?"

"Trying to keep you out of the hospital," he answered grimly. "So shut up and strip."

Four

"**T**ake your hands off me!"

Gabe ignored her. He lifted her shirt over her head, then reached for the snap at her waistband. Weak as she was, she had the gumption to take a swipe at him. Her blow landed against his chest with all the force of a gnat.

"Look, I'm just trying to help," he said, pushing her jeans down her slender hips, then sliding them and her tennis shoes off in one movement.

He wasn't surprised to discover that her underthings were plain, utilitarian cotton. Practical, responsible garments, in keeping with her personality—and as revealing as a second skin in their sweat-dampened state.

Her gasp was a sob of fury. "I don't want your help, you big gorilla!"

"Tough."

He lifted her into the tub and shoved her under the luke-warm spray, holding her there. Her shriek was accompa-

nied by a flow of invective that would have made his former
Ranger buddies grin in admiration.

"Good gravy, ma'am, where'd you learn such lan-
guage?"

"I'll kill you for this." Black hair slicked back, rivulets
pouring over her shoulders, she clenched her fists and
glared at him with murder in her eye. Water dripped off the
tip of her nose. "Someday, somewhere, slowly, painfully..."

"Feeling better?" Splattered and half-soaked himself, he
chuckled, admiring the picture she made, spitting and mad
as a wet kitten.

Then his gaze sharpened. Her cotton bra and panties
were all but transparent under the shower's spray, revealing the enticing shadow at the juncture of her thighs,
sculpting the surprisingly heavy fullness of her breasts. As
he watched, her nipples puckered under the translucent
fabric, rosy crests in impudent relief, daring a man to
touch, to taste, to savor.

Images exploded in his head—pictures of his joining her
beneath that warm spray, exploring with his fingers the
slick silkiness of her skin, plumbing the hidden mysteries of
her body. Fire shot through his loins, and his belly tightened.

She stifled a gasp and crossed her arms defensively. "Get
out!"

"Yeah," he agreed, releasing her. His voice was thick.
"That might be a good idea."

"Out!" Red-faced, she fumbled to shut off the water.

He tossed a navy-and-yellow-striped towel to her, re-
gretfully watching her restore her modesty. "That cooled
you off, at least."

Dragging the towel around her, she spluttered in indignation. "I'm not the one who needs a cold shower, mister!"

From the throbbing in his lower body, Gabe couldn't argue that point. He paused at the door, surveying her. "Holler for me if you think you're going to pass out again."

"I'd rather die."

"Well, try to avoid that while we're still legally husband and wife, will you? Too many awkward questions."

A bath brush sailed past his ear. He retreated into the hallway to an even more colorful string of Sarah Ann's curses, then stood grinning to himself. Damn, the woman was full of surprises, from her devil's tongue to her angel's body.

It was a good thing she wanted to feed him to the buzzards, because given the least bit of encouragement, he might have succumbed to that surge of unbridled lust. Hell, he was just a man, after all, and a hungry one. Under other circumstances, a little sexual free-for-all might have been a quick and easy solution to the age-old problem of the chemistry that was brewing between them.

Gabe rubbed his nape and grimaced. And brewing it was, with a vengeance, whether he liked to admit it or not. Which left him with a big ache, and an even bigger problem—keeping his distance before his hormones led him into some damned tomfoolery with a stubborn slip of a woman who was his wife but shouldn't be.

He frowned again. A woman who obviously didn't know her own limits. A woman who worked so hard she lost sight of reality, not to mention safety. A woman who, despite a flare of temper and a cool bath, was certainly in no condition to spend hours at the hospital tonight with her sick grandfather. Since he'd rescued her from that damned roof, he felt responsible. The least he could do was see she didn't overdo it any further.

Minutes later, Gabe was on the kitchen phone talking with Harlan.

"Yes, sir, that's what I said, the roof. And she was already a bit under the weather."

"Lord, what am I going to do with that girl?" The old man's voice crackled through the wire.

"She's a stubborn one," Gabe agreed. He stretched the phone cord while he poked among the contents of the cabinets, unearthing a loaf of whole wheat bread and some tea bags.

"But you love her, don't you, son?"

Gabe's hand hesitated halfway to the teakettle. Resolutely he filled it under the sink faucet and set it on the stove. "Would I have married her otherwise?"

"You see how she is. You see the condition of the place. She's been killing herself taking care of it, slaving her life away for an old man's dreams."

"Sarah Ann cares about this farm, Harlan."

"But she sacrificed her college to pitch in, and then that bastard, Roy, broke their engagement over it."

That startled Gabe. So she'd had someone special before. Why did that unsettle him?

With an old man's garrulousness, Harlan rambled on. "And she ain't had much of a social life, or time for friends, except maybe Merrilee Stratton down at the Stop 'N Go. After Sarah Ann's folks were killed, she and I were everything to each other. She's not the kind of woman who ought to be alone. So I can die happy knowing you're going to be the one taking care of her from now on. I'm counting on you, Gabe Thornton. I got no one else to depend on."

Gabe cleared his throat, shifting his boots uncomfortably. "Yes, sir. I understand. I'll do my best."

It was part of the bargain, for him to make these promises to Harlan, all part of the lie that he and Sarah Ann were trapped inside. Gabe wondered how he could feel any sense of obligation for pledges made under these conditions, yet somehow he did. It was disturbing. He'd have to work on getting over it.

"Well, you keep Sarah Ann right there at home tonight," Harlan ordered. "Tell her I'm doing fine—except for the new nurse who's been tormenting me all blasted day."

"Someone giving you a hard time?"

"Big ugly gal. Bossy, too. Ordering a man to get well like that. It ain't Christian."

Gabe chuckled, reaching for the kettle that had just begun to whistle. He poured hot water into a mug holding a tea bag. "Don't you worry, sir. We'll see you tomorrow. But tonight I'm going to send Sarah Ann to bed with tea and toast."

Harlan's quivery laugh was rife with skepticism. "Then you're a better man than I am, son. Good luck." He hung up.

"I hate tea. I despise toast. And I'm not going to bed."

Gabe spun on his heel to find Sarah Ann in the kitchen doorway, wrapped in a faded seersucker housecoat, her hair combed back but already beginning to dry into beguiling tendrils at her temples. She was still too pale, her eyes too wide, but her expression was obstinate. Defiant. Valiant. Adorable.

And it struck Gabe that he wanted her like hell.

In a day filled with frustrations and false promises, lust and lies, it was too much.

With a growl, he grabbed her, ignoring her squeak of surprise, then hustled her into the adjoining family room and plunked her into a cushiony club chair. Barely in control, he kicked the matching ottoman into place and placed her feet on it. Wide-eyed, Sarah Ann gripped the arms of the chair, ready to bolt.

He pointed a finger at her nose. "Don't move."

He retrieved the mug and a plateful of toast from the kitchen and set it at her elbow.

"You *will* drink that tea," he said, his voice low and ominous. "With as much sugar as you can stomach."

"No, I won't."

He leaned closer, his eyes going narrow and dangerous. "You *will* eat that toast. Every crumb."

Her chin went up. "Uh-uh."

Placing his hands on the chair arms next to hers, he bent over her, nose to nose, forcing her back against the cushions. "And you *will* go to bed."

"No. I'm not a child. You can't make me."

"You're right about one thing," he said, staring at her mouth. Nervously she licked her lips, and he nearly groaned. "You're definitely not a child. But I can make you go to bed. With me. And we both know it."

She inhaled sharply, shaking her head in denial. "No, I—"

"So if you don't want me to forget about consequences, carry you to your bed and keep us both there until neither of us can walk, you'd better humor me. Any questions?"

Her eyes were purple with rebellion, and a part of Gabe welcomed it, yearned for the excuse to touch her again, but when she spoke her voice was small.

"Is there any jelly for the toast?"

"Gramps seems weaker."

"Yes."

Sarah Ann drew a tremulous breath at Gabe's reply, staring out the windshield as he guided his Jeep away from the hospital the next evening. The summer twilights were growing ever longer, but by this time of the day it was quiet in Lostman's Island.

The only activity of any note was a family she recognized from church entering Tacky's Ice Cream Parlor. The teenage daughter poked her mother, pointing toward the Jeep as they passed. Sarah Ann wondered absently if it were the shiny vehicle or the man driving who caught their attention.

Farther down the street, store manager Louis Edwards was busy taking in the displays of half-inflated rubber rafts, sunglasses and straw hats from in front of the Ben Franklin Five and Dime. When they pulled up to the stoplight in front of the store, he noticed Sarah Ann and waved brightly to her, a curious gesture from a man whose arms were loaded with water floats in the shapes of dolphins and alligators. Puzzled, she returned the wave.

As Gabe put the Jeep in gear again, she chanced another look at him, then asked the question that was preying most on her mind.

"Do you think Gramps has given up?"

"Hard to say."

"Now that he's sure I'll be okay, do you think he might stop trying?"

"It's possible."

Guilt clogged her throat. "Then I've made things worse."

"Could be."

It wasn't what she wanted to hear, that fulfilling Gramps's dearest wish about his granddaughter's future had taken away his will to live.

"How can I bear to lose him?" she murmured.

"You just will."

Gabe's phlegmatic reply set her teeth on edge, but she controlled the urge to take umbrage. Since their explosive encounter the previous evening, she and Gabe had both backed off from further confrontation, but if his laconic-Texan's replies grew any shorter, he'd be speaking in grunts instead of merely monosyllables. As it was, he'd hardly said a word during their obligatory visit to Gramps, other than to be cordial, and she knew that the subterfuge as well as the tension between them made him as uncomfortable as it did her.

And it was a tension that could have been avoided, or at least ignored, if the blasted man hadn't put it into such vivid terms! Sarah Ann swallowed hard on a lump of embarrassment. Could she help it that Gabe Thornton had such animal magnetism her female libido jumped into overdrive whenever he was in the vicinity? Surely there were other men who looked as good in tight jeans and cowboy boots? Plenty of other guys had muscular shoulders that filled out a knit shirt with breath-stopping perfection and biceps that rippled like steel cords.

It was simply that she was in such a vulnerable, highly charged emotional state at the moment, that was all, she told herself firmly. And he certainly wasn't much of a gentleman to notice her involuntary reaction to all those male pheromones, much less mention it, either! But he had, and even if it had simply been to shock her into compliance, she couldn't shake the images his blunt words had evoked.

Images of bodies pressed close. Of mouths clinging sweetly. Of exploration and carnality and heat. All wrong. All forbidden. And oh, so tempting.

She smoothed her tailored twill shorts, pressing her hands hard against her thighs to still their trembling. Despite the vehicle's air-conditioning and her cool eyelet blouse, beads of moisture popped out on her upper lip and in the hollow between her breasts, breasts which still felt itchy and sensitive. Drawing a deep breath, she gripped her thighs harder.

She might be a fool, but not so great a one as to think anything good or lasting could happen with a lone wolf like Gabe Thornton. She had to get control of herself! And the only way to do it was to put distance between herself and the source of her confusion. The sooner Gabe dropped her off at home, the better.

Near the edge of town, he pulled the Jeep up to the fuel pumps at the tiny Stop 'N Go Grocery and Convenience Store.

"Gas."

She reflected sourly that he was down to single-word communication now. What next, Morse code? "Of course."

Business at the Stop 'N Go in gas, last-minute milk and bread, and broasted chicken dinners was brisk. Idly, Sarah Ann watched the comings and goings while Gabe pumped his gas. She recognized a trio of schoolteachers on their way to evening classes in Ft. Myers, each carrying a drink in a paper cup and a chicken box. They nodded to Gabe as he went inside to pay, then smiled in Sarah Ann's direction before hopping into their vehicle and speeding off.

All this friendliness made her vaguely uneasy. She sat up straighter, craning her neck, and found that she could just see Gabe at the inside counter paying the cashier—her friend, Merrilee Stratton. Hastily, Sarah Ann scrunched down in the seat, making herself as small as possible. The last thing she wanted was curious questions from Merrilee.

It struck her how ludicrous her actions were, and she stifled a humorless laugh. Didn't she have enough to worry about with Gramps without becoming paranoid, too? *How did I get myself into this?* Hiding from her friends, lying to an old man, playing dangerous games with a soldier-of-fortune she didn't even know! With a groan, she shut her eyes, praying that somehow it would all be over soon.

"Hey, are you okay?"

Sarah Ann jerked upright as Gabe slid in behind the wheel. "Sure. Fine. Just a little tired."

He frowned, then started the Jeep and pulled out onto the highway. "Still feeling the aftereffects of that little stunt of yours, I'll wager. And by the way, don't get back up on that roof. I'll be by tomorrow to finish it up—"

"You needn't bother." Her voice was stiff. "I took care of it."

His expression turned ominous. "The hell you say."

She bristled. "This morning. Not that it's any of your business."

"So you keep telling me. So what else did you do today? Hog-tie a bull elephant and drink Lake Michigan?"

"Sarcasm doesn't become you. As a matter of fact, Tony and I pulled the engine on the little tractor."

"Tony?"

"My hired hand."

"So you will accept some help occasionally. Amazing. And that explains this." He grabbed her hand, turning it palm up to inspect the abrasions heavy machinery was wont to inflict. His expression grew even darker. "Trying to prove you're Superwoman, huh?"

"I have nothing to prove to anyone." Breaking free, she closed her fingers over the incriminating scratches, and her tone became imperious. "Unlike some people, I have work to do, responsibilities. I don't have time to laze the day away in a hammock."

"Maybe that's your problem." His foot pressed the accelerator and the Jeep hurtled down the flat, two-lane highway. A salty tang drifted off Paradise Bay. "And you haven't lived until you've made love in a hammock, ma'am."

She choked. "The only problem I've got is your insufferable attitude and intolerable behavior, Gabe Thornton. And the sooner I can see the last of you, the better I'll like it!"

"Shucks, ma'am," he drawled. "All that sweet talk's going right to my head."

With a disgusted flounce, she turned toward the passenger window. "Just take me home."

"So you can plow the north forty before dawn?"

Sarah Ann thought about the pile of bills to pay, the laundry to do, the endless list of household chores that always had to wait until after dark, but she'd be damned if she'd give him the satisfaction of picking on her because she was swamped.

"No, so that I can get my dinner and go to—" After the previous night's confrontation, she balked at the word *bed*.

But he picked up on something else entirely. "You haven't eaten? Since when?"

She blinked, taken off guard. "I don't know. Breakfast, I guess."

"Damnation, woman, you need a keeper!"

"Now you sound like Gramps."

"He and I appear to have a lot more in common than I thought."

"Well, you don't have to worry—hey, you missed my road!" Dismayed, she watched her turnoff fly by in the twilight. "Turn around."

"Forget it. I'm taking you to Angel's Landing so Beulah can feed you. And me, too, while she's at it."

"Of all the high-handed, arrogant, insufferable—"

"Stow it, Sarah Ann. Maybe I can keep you from work-ing yourself into a stupor for one more night, at least."

"It's not your place."

He thrust a restless hand through his sandy hair and glowered at her. "Temporarily, it seems it is. So you may as well shut up and enjoy the ride."

She was so furious she sputtered. "Did anyone ever tell you that you're a tyrant? It's a wonder all your troops didn't mutiny."

Gabe peeled to a stop on the shells in front of Angel's Landing. Grinning, he hauled her out of the Jeep and marched her into the main building where the air was red-olent with tantalizing cooking aromas. "What makes you think they didn't?"

Dazzled by the brightly lit room, she hissed under her breath. "I'd like to get you in front of a firing squad, Gabe Thornton!"

"Lookit what the cat dragged in, will ya?" Beulah stood in the kitchen doorway, waving a spatula at the wreath of cigarette smoke that haloed her head.

"About time you showed up, Cap'n." The wiry man with a jet black ponytail unfolded himself from a lounge chair.

"Yeah, always knew you were a closemouthed, secre-tive SOB." Another man with red, curly hair crossed the room with a glass in his hand. "But this takes the cake."

Sarah Ann froze at the sight of Gabe's partners. Gabe squeezed her arm in warning.

"Mind your manners, Gabriel," Beulah snapped. "In-troduce the lady."

Gabe cleared his throat. "Uh, Sarah Ann, Rafe Okee and Mike Hennesey."

"Flat broke our hearts to have to hear the news on the streets," Mike said, his tone mournful, but his blue eyes teasing. "How long were you planning to keep it from us?"

"Keep what?" Gabe asked cautiously.

"Come on now, Cap'n, don't be coy." Rafe's brilliant white grin split his dark face. "The whole town's buzzing about the most romantic wedding in Lostman's Island in years."

"Oh, no." Dismayed, Sarah Ann flicked Gabe an apprehensive glance. Everyone knew? Even after they'd done their best to keep things quiet?

"The whole town?" Gabe's sandy brows lowered in a ferocious scowl. "How—?"

"Heard it at the Stop 'N Go, myself," Rafe said.

Beulah nodded. "Post office."

Mike grinned. "Hardware store."

Gabe groaned. "Damnation."

"Swept the little lady right off her feet, by all accounts," Rafe said. "Never would have thought a beat-up old warrior like you capable of such a thing."

"Must have hidden depths." Laughing, Mike advanced with his hand extended. "Congratulations, partner. And, Sarah Ann, welcome. We're pleased as punch."

She caught Gabe's glance, then swallowed hard at the furious, cornered light behind his tawny eyes. She held her breath. What would he do?

His jaw tight, he accepted Mike's handshake. "It, uh, took us both by surprise."

"'Bout time something woke you up," Beulah muttered, smirking at the glare he sent her way.

Sarah Ann didn't know whether to laugh in relief that Gabe hadn't revealed the truth or cry in despair that they'd have to persist with the falsehood to an even higher level of deception. Every step was like trying to dog-paddle through

quicksand, sinking deeper and deeper the more they struggled.

"I'm just glad you finally decided to bring the lady home
to meet the folks," Rafe said.

"Me, too." Mike grinned at Sarah Ann, then dropped a
quick peck on her cheek. "She gets my stamp of approval."

"And an award for valor," Rafe quipped. "Break out
our best bottle of hooch, Beulah. Let's toast the first Fallen
Angel to take a bride!"

Somehow, it turned into a party.

Beulah appeared with trays of hors d'oeuvres—hot sea-
food dips, sliced honeydew melons and sweetened sour
cream, pastry puffs around paper-thin roast beef—and announced there just weren't enough people to do her culinary efforts justice. A few phone calls produced a group of
Mike's lady friends, as well as Merrilee and two other clerks
from the Stop 'N Go coming off the early-evening shift.
Judge Holt drove up with Evelyn Travis, a widow he'd been
seeing, and the Watsons, an elderly couple who'd been
friends with Gramps since the old days. Even Tony Man-
sur, Sarah Ann's hired man, showed up with his wife and
three teenage sons to offer congratulations.

Someone had turned on some music, and the conversation flowed freely, along with a rather fine Beaujolais,
which Mike had uncorked with due solemnity as part of the
toasting and celebration. It was all very tasteful, just right
for an impromptu reception for the happy couple, considering the unusual circumstances of their whirlwind courtship and the seriousness of Harlan's condition.

Laid-back. Elegant, in a casual way. Friendly.

And absolutely excruciating for the new bride and
groom.

Wound tight as a spring, Sarah Ann pretended an interest she didn't feel in a toast point covered with Caribbean mango chutney and attempted to dodge another question.

"Known each other long?" Merrilee asked. Still clad in her pink work overall, the stocky brunette's brown eyes sparkled with good wishes and curiosity.

"No, not long," Sarah Ann replied weakly.

"Honestly, I could kill you for not even giving me a hint!"

She shrugged. "It happened so fast . . ."

Merrilee gave a mock pout. "I guess I'll forgive you, this time. I couldn't have said no, either, not when the man's obviously so crazy about you."

Gabe stood nearby, his fair head gleaming as he bent to address a knockout blonde clinging to Mike's arm. Sarah Ann's stomach lurched, and she set the toast point aside uneaten.

"Yes," she murmured, "*crazy* is the perfect word."

"Yup, one of those crazy things, I guess," Gabe said to Mike and the woman. He made his expression unreadable, but his stomach was in knots. This good-meaning quizzing was worse than an enemy interrogation!

"So you went to talk about frontage property, and something between you and the lady just clicked," Mike surmised. His look was part admiration, part envy. "Man, I never thought of you as impulsive, but when you know it's right . . ."

"I just have to look at you to know you're right for each other," Merrilee said enthusiastically to Sarah Ann. "Where are you going to live?"

Sarah Ann's heart turned over. Live? With Gabe? But that's what married couples did, didn't they? That's what all these people would expect Gabe and her to do, too. Why hadn't that occurred to her until now?

She reached for her glass and took a swallow of ice water—no wine for her; she'd learned her lesson! "Uh, we haven't decided. Things are so up in the air." She glanced over at Gabe.

Rafe had just joined them. "A pretty woman like that can sure blow a man right out of the air," he said, clapping Gabe on the shoulder. "Right, Cap'n?"

"Uh, yeah." Tension churning his belly, Gabe looked for an avenue of retreat. "Excuse me, I think Sarah Ann needs some..."

"Air," Sarah Ann gasped, fighting a sense of overwhelming panic. "Sorry, Merrilee. I'll be back."

Blindly seeking escape, she made her way toward the rear French doors. Gabe materialized beside her, reaching for the doorknob before she could.

"Where do you think you're going?" His voice was harsh.

"Just out. It's...I..."

He wrenched open the door and thrust her through it. "Yeah, me, too."

The fragrance of bougainvillea and hibiscus sweetened the moist night air. Lit only by a security light at the end of the property, the path leading to the bungalows danced with shadows.

Sarah Ann's tennis shoes crunched on the shells, and she came up short under the canopy of faintly clattering palm trees, surprised to find that she was trembling. "I don't know if I can do this."

"It's too late for that now." Disgust etched his words with acid. "Well, so much for the low profile. You've gotten us well and truly in the soup this time."

"Me?" She clenched her fists, her temper rising. "I'm not the one who insisted on dragging me over here tonight. Your friends—"

"Hell, it's not their fault everybody and his cat knows about us—or thinks they do. But that means we have to play the part to the hilt or risk blowing the whole thing wide open. And if that—" he indicated the party inside the building with a jerk of his head "—is any indication of what I can expect, I'd rather face an entire regiment of bloodthirsty mercenaries."

"What do you care?" she demanded, her tone scathing. "You don't even know these people! I'm the one who's lived here all my life. I'll have to face them again after you're out of the picture. There goes Sarah Ann, they'll say. Remember her? What kind of lunatic marries a man she's known only days? Serves her right for being such a fool."

"Why worry about your reputation at this point? Besides, I thought you would bargain with the devil for Harlan's sake."

"It wasn't supposed to be like this. And I didn't bargain for *you,* so you leave Gramps out of it." At the mention of her grandfather, her throat constricted with the promise of tears. Too furious to let them come, she shouted at him instead. "You're no prize, you know. Always bellowing at me. Ordering me around. Making decisions you have no right to make. You're a *terrible* husband!"

Gabe glanced toward the doorway. "Stop it. People will hear."

"Worried they'll think we're having a lovers' spat?" She tossed her head, glaring up at him. "Just think of it as groundwork for the breakup of our marriage. Now nobody will be surprised. Pretty smart, huh?"

Then to her utter chagrin, the tears spilled over.

His expression changed, and he reached for her. "Sarah—"

"No." Choking, she turned and stumbled down the path, not knowing where she was going, only that she had to get

away from him, from the confusing, tumultuous feelings
of loss and longing that were turning her into a person she
didn't even recognize.

She didn't get far.

Gabe caught her shoulders, molding her to his side to
control her feeble attempts at escape. Cursing under his
breath, he hesitated, then led her toward a weathered clapboard bungalow. "Sarah, honey, stop."

"Why can't you leave me alone?" Her voice caught on
a sob. "I don't want to be anywhere near you!"

"Tough. Come inside my place until you calm down."

He guided her inside the cottage, flipping on the light to
reveal a spare and military-neat apartment—sitting room,
bedroom, bath—books stacked in regimental rows on the
shelves, a high-tech music system, but few pictures or personal items, except for a Western landscape on one wall
over a battered leather sofa.

"I'm calm enough to know I'm sick of you, Gabe
Thornton!" Cheeks wet, she pushed at his chest, struggling to break free of the circle of his arms.

"Shh. I know you are." He rubbed her back, soothing
her with his warm hands, his expression remorseful. "I'm
sorry. My temper..."

She shook her head, unwilling to be placated, the tears
slipping from her lashes one by one, her breaths coming
short and painful. "Why are you such a bully?"

"Force of habit. I'm accustomed to giving orders, you
know."

The hint of humor in his words undid her anger, left her
defenseless. She looked up at him, at the strength and concern in his face, and her lower lip trembled violently. "And
Gramps. I'm so scared."

"I know, sweetheart, I know. We all are."

And somehow she could see that he did know, that in another life he'd faced death countless times himself and led others into the midst of it. Maybe the way he guarded himself emotionally was the result of that, but all she knew at this moment was that for the briefest of instants, he'd lowered a wall and let her peep over it.

All the fight went out of her then, swept aside by a sob that rose from her depths, and she collapsed against Gabe's broad chest. His arms tightened around her, supporting her as he eased them both down on the sofa, cradling her protectively as she wept.

"I'm sorry, Gabriel." Her fingers twisted the fabric of his shirt. "Sorry I'm such a witch to you."

"You've been through a lot."

"I know you didn't ask for this mess."

"No, it's all right. No one's fault."

"I haven't even thanked you."

"It's okay." He smoothed her hair back and kissed her on the forehead. "We'll work it out. Somehow, we'll..."

He trailed off, gazing down at her tear-glazed features. Almost of their own volition, his fingers came up to trace the wet tracks on her cheeks, smoothing them away. He dipped his head again, using his tongue to taste the lingering salt at the corner of her eye, the curve of her cheek, the soft edge of her mouth. She caught her breath.

"Don't cry," he murmured. "Sarah..."

And she couldn't, because then his lips settled over hers, sweetly, softly, in a kiss so tender it stole her sorrow away and left only the utter completeness of his possession to enthrall her. Gently he fed her strength and comfort with the warmth of his caress, and when she sighed and parted her lips it wasn't in surrender, but, rather, in a fulfillment of what they shared ... together.

Leisurely Gabe explored her mouth, his tongue taking nimble liberties. Tentative, uncertain, but drawn by a force that compelled her to respond, Sarah Ann touched the tip of her tongue to his, and was rewarded with his groan of pleasure. Strangely elated, she raised her hand to stroke his cheek, exulting in the texture of male skin raspy with golden stubble.

He was so very *alive,* so vital he filled up her senses to the brim. A hard man, but capable of tenderness, of giving. She trembled all over again, not with an excess of nerves, but with a sense of burgeoning need she barely understood.

They drew apart at last, and dazed violet eyes met fiery golden ones. Wondering, unsure, they held time and reason suspended in a cocoon of sweet sensation. She could have reached for him then, could have turned it into something different in that moment, something more potent and dazzling and urgent, but then Gabe's expression flickered, both revelation and withdrawal. He drew a shuddering breath, as if he were in great pain, and tore his gaze free.

Without a word he straightened and tucked her against his chest, holding her in a fashion that could only be described as brotherly. Stunned, Sarah Ann sat still while her judgment returned and chagrin replaced insanity.

When he finally spoke, his voice was gruff. "We'll work something out."

She couldn't look at him, could only nod, and she fervently prayed that the earth would open and hell consume her before she ever came this close to making such a fool of herself again.

The door of the bungalow opened and closed, and a man and a woman walked slowly toward the parking lot of Angel's Landing, keeping a careful distance between them.

Deep in the shadows, a henna haired woman watched closely. The tip of her cigarette glowed, then made a sparkling, comet-tailed arc against the night sky. A heavy sigh, a single smoky comment.

"Jerk."

Five

───

"I told you before, you don't have to do this."

Arrested by the sight of Gabe's bare, tanned back bent over the innards of her ailing tractor, Sarah Ann blurted the protest, then instantly regretted her shrewish tone. A mysterious collection of oily engine parts spilled onto the tarp at his feet, mute evidence of his afternoon's labor in the shady equipment shed, and more fodder for her growing burden of guilt.

Gabe straightened, giving her a full and heart-stopping view of his muscular chest, damp with sweat and streaked with black smudges of grease. "My charter flight fell through."

"But—"

Grimacing, he tossed the wrench he held into an open toolbox and reached for a rag to wipe his hands. "I've got the time. I know engines. What's the problem?"

Feeling like the most ungracious whelp in the world, Sarah Ann made a self-conscious swipe at the curls escaping her topknot and attempted to smooth the wrinkles in her navy linen pants and vest. The problem wasn't her rumpled appearance after an afternoon's business in town, however. No, it was the fact that in the four days since their celebration party at Angel's Landing, Gabe Thornton had made himself entirely too useful around the Dempsey place.

A thousand and one routine maintenance chores that Sarah Ann had been forced to put on hold due to Gramps's illness and sheer lack of time and manpower had been accomplished virtually overnight. Fences mended, irrigation ditches cleared, equipment overhauled, fallow tomato fields cultivated—there was even a fresh coat of paint on the front porch!

Of course, to the outside world, it was simply a new bridegroom pitching in where he was needed, and his actions certainly gave the stamp of authenticity to their "marriage." Thank God no one seemed to notice that Gabe still spent his nights at his bungalow at Angel's Landing. Or that the real reason he was so intent on performing chore after chore despite any protest she mounted was that it was payback time for involving him in this out-and-out lie.

It was obvious he was trying to drive her crazy. The worst part was, he was succeeding.

Even now, the sight of him, half-naked and magnificent in just a pair of low-slung jeans, made her palms sweat and her mouth go dry. She stifled an inward groan, willing her racing heart to calmness, trying to cool the sweet rush of heat that filled her. She could more easily have stopped the tide rising and falling in Paradise Bay.

It was maddening. It was embarrassing. And after their last encounter, it was abundantly clear that it was the last thing Gabe needed or wanted—at least from her. Chagrin clogged her throat, and her feminine self-esteem hit rock bottom at the memory of his rejection.

Taking a breath, Sarah Ann grappled with her wayward emotions. All right, so Gabe had proven not only that he was a championship kisser, but that he could be compassionate and tender, too. But she'd accidentally trapped the man into this farce of a marriage. Until they were free of each other, the least she could do was spare Gabe the embarrassment of her schoolgirl crush! And spare herself the humiliation of losing her head with him again, only to have him turn her down cold.

That's why she needed to see less of Gabe, not more of him, and his sweeping in and taking over her turf wasn't helping at all! But stopping Gabe was like walking into the path of a runaway bulldozer.

"It's not that I'm not grateful," she said weakly, "but I can't take even more advantage..."

Gabe gave a snort. "Of what? My good nature? We both know I don't have one, so give it a rest."

He walked to the faucet at the shed entrance and turned on the hose, sluicing water over his chest and head. Sarah Ann glanced at the pile of parts, then at his strong, work-stained hands.

"As the recipient of your recent good works, I can't totally buy that."

Grinning, he shook his wet hair out of his face and raised the nozzle in a mock threat. "Want me to pull something despicable and prove it to you?"

Her lips twitched. "I'm also beginning to believe that your bark is worse than your bite, just like Gramps."

His expression darkened. "You're too damned trusting."

She looked from the gushing water nozzle to his face. "Am I?"

After a long moment the corner of his mouth twisted in a self-deprecating grimace. Shrugging, he dropped the hose and turned off the water.

"Maybe you're just lucky today, sweetheart. At any rate, don't give me any extra credit for helping out around here a little."

"I can at least say thanks and offer you something cold to drink, can't I?"

Now why did I do that? She mentally kicked herself for not hurrying him on his way so that her pulse could return to normal. Still, the man had been laboring over a hot engine all afternoon, and common courtesy demanded some concessions.

Gabe shrugged into his chambray shirt, leaving it unbuttoned for coolness. "The drink sounds good, but save your gratitude. We agreed to keep up appearances, didn't we? Besides, this place kind of reminds me of home."

She fell into step beside him, and they walked toward the house. "Texas?"

"A ranch near Austin. My folks are still there."

"Do you see them very much?"

"Not as often as they'd like."

"Why's that?"

Gabe held the porch door open for her, his expression mocking. "You know what they say about curiosity, ma'am."

"I know you 'ma'am' me whenever you want to dodge a question." She led him into the shabby, yet cheerful, yellow kitchen, pointing out soap and dish towels as she went to the refrigerator. "You can wash up while you tell me why you stay away."

He lathered his hands at the old enamel sink. As he reached for a towel, his jaw tightened. "It's hard, that's all. There are things they don't know..."

"I know they must be very proud of you."

He went very still, then turned to her, pain burning behind his tawny eyes. "No," he said, his voice husky, "I don't think that's it."

"Then you're wrong, Gabriel," she said simply. Handing him a tall glass of iced tea laced with lemon and mint, she lifted her own tumbler in a salute. "Cheers."

His fingers clenched around the dewy glass, and annoyance hardened his features. "Don't make up fairy tales about me, Pollyanna. It'll only get you in trouble."

She gave a rueful laugh. "I'd say I'm there already."

"No luck at the bank?"

"On the contrary. They were very... cooperative." Sighing, she sat down in a captain's chair at the scarred pine breakfast table, fished the wedge of lemon from her tea and chewed it thoughtfully. "We'll have to refinance, of course, if we're ever to replant the orchards, but I think the tomatoes will save us there. We'll squeak by somehow, if nothing else happens. And then there's the hospital bills... but I'm sure it will all work out."

"Keeping this place alive is a mighty tall order for a woman alone."

Startled, she realized she was still unconsciously operating on the assumption that Gramps would always be around. Gabe's blunt reminder of the inevitable made her heart sink in her chest. And for all of his casual and quite welcome help, Gabe would be gone soon, too. Fighting a renewed sense of dismay, she took a steadying breath and lifted her chin. "I can do it. I have to. The Dempsey legacy is Gramps's dream."

"What about your dreams? Isn't it time you thought about what Sarah Ann wants?"

"It's the same thing."

Setting his empty glass in the sink, he leaned a hip against the cabinet and cocked a sandy eyebrow at her. "Is it? What about the things every woman wants—a husband, a family? Are you sacrificing that kind of life out of misplaced loyalty? Do you really think that's what Harlan wants?"

His words pricked her in her most vulnerable spot. Yes, she yearned for a loving family, a committed relationship, a happily-ever-after future. But life hadn't provided those opportunities, so she was making do by preserving her heritage and home the best she could. It might not be enough, but at least it was something of her own, an Gabe had no right to question her decision.

She scowled at him. "My motives are none of your concern."

"Since they've led you to extremes no sane person would consider, and since I'm up to my eyeballs in the consequences of those extremes, I'd say you're wrong."

"Well, your involvement is limited, so it doesn't make any real difference, does it?" she asked, belligerent. She rose and went to move past him. "Excuse me, I've got to get to the hospital."

"Touched a nerve, did I?" Gabe caught her by the nape of the neck, bringing her to a halt beside him.

The warmth of his hand and the wide expanse of his bare chest made her catch her breath. "Don't toy with me!"

"No." His thumb made lazy, soothing circles in the hollow behind her ear. "Look, I'll buy you supper and then we'll both go see Harlan, okay?"

Rattled by his nearness, the heady scents of soap and masculine musk, she shook her head. Hadn't she decided her only defense against this man's charisma was distance? And she didn't want to face any more of his pointed questions, either. "That's not necessary."

"Don't give me a hard time. We both have to eat, and it'll get you to the hospital sooner rather than later."

"But I'm a mess—"

"And I'm dirty. So what?" He gave her a lopsided grin, and devilment sparkled in his eyes. "Mess or not, you're gorgeous, and the gossips will chalk up our frazzled appearances to a hot and heavy honeymoon."

Crimson flooded her cheeks. "You—you've got to stop saying things like that. This is business—"

A frown replaced his smile. "You really have no idea, do you?"

"Idea?"

"That I'm having a hell of a time keeping my mitts off you."

She drew a shaky breath. "Gabe, please. We really don't need to discuss this."

"When a woman doesn't even realize how desirable she is, apparently we do." He tugged her into place between his boots, and his words rasped harshly. "When she can't even tell that a man would ransom his soul for another chance to touch, to taste . . ."

His fingers stroked her neck, then explored the hollow at the base of her throat where her pulse leapt. Mesmerized, she watched his expression grow more intense, his eyes more golden, as he investigated the silkiness of her skin. But then that wasn't enough for him any longer. Without warning he undid the top button on her vest, sliding his hand inside to cup the lush fullness of her breast. Sarah Ann gasped, both shocked and pleasured.

She swayed, catching herself with her hands against his hair-dusted chest, shivering at the intimate contact, her whisper raw. "Gabe, we shouldn't . . ."

He gave a tortured groan. "God help me, I have to."

With that, he captured her mouth. His lips were hard, unyielding, his possession powerful and utterly exciting. Liquid fire sizzled through Sarah Ann's veins, melting her core, dissolving her knees. If there was any doubt left in her mind about the power of his need, it vanished completely when he dragged her close and she felt the hard ridge of his arousal pressing against her. His fingers explored the puckered rose of her nipple though her thin cotton bra, and she whimpered against his lips.

When he raised his head, his breath came in gusts, and his expression was almost savage. "You see what you can do to a man? Never doubt yourself again."

"But the other night, you didn't—" She broke off, shaking her head in bewilderment.

"Because I'm not the one for you, don't you understand?" Reluctantly, almost angrily, he released her, setting her away as though she were the embodiment of all temptation. "I've got nothing to give anymore, if I ever did."

Desire died in Sarah Ann, its heat replaced by an Arctic chill of fury. Backing away, she fumbled with her buttons, her voice icy. "Your presumption is exceeded only by your arrogance."

Gabe scrubbed the back of his sun-streaked head in frustration. "Don't be naive. We both know what's going on here. We've got the hots for each other big-time, but even if the legal circumstances were different, sex is still a major mistake."

Knuckles white, Sarah Ann grasped the back of a kitchen chair for support and arrowed a scathing look straight through his heart. "Is that what that little demonstration was all about? Well, you've certainly proven your point. Congratulations."

"Don't get your nose out of joint, woman," he growled. "It would be fantastic between us. You go up in flames when I touch you, and I'm on the verge of exploding like a green kid all the time. All I can think about is how good it would be to have you beneath me."

Her breath caught at the carnal image. "Stop it."

"Hell, that's what I'm trying to do!" he snapped. He blew out an unsteady breath, wrestling for control, and his tone softened. "I know it wouldn't be something casual to a woman like you, Sarah."

Stung, perversely hurt by his assessment even though it was true, she glared at him, sarcasm turning her tone to acid. "Oh, is that why you're being so very noble?"

"Look, you need a man who can be there for you, not a burnt-out ex-soldier like me. And you'll find one, if you don't bury yourself on this damned farm for the rest of your life!"

"You haven't the faintest idea what I need," she replied coldly. "And I'm entitled to make my own mistakes, so keep your damned-fool advice to yourself, mister."

He threw up his hands. "Fine. Just trying to help."

"Help? Then from now on, remember this is a business arrangement, nothing more. Are we clear on that?"

Jaw taut, Gabe crossed his arms. "Yes, ma'am."

Humiliated, insulted, Sarah Ann realized that she'd let pure animal attraction cloud the real issue, make her forget what was really at stake in this whole mess. It wouldn't happen again.

She lifted her chin, damned if she'd show him any further weakness. "I want to be at the hospital when the doctor makes his rounds. Are you coming?"

"Might as well." Gabe shrugged, his eyes hooded, his smile mocking, as if he'd read her determination and knew just how futile it was. "After all, it's just business."

* * *

He'd never seen a woman seethe like this one before. She was a volcano in imminent danger of eruption. A tigress rabid to rip the throat from her prey. A star ready to go nova and consume everything in its vicinity in flame and fury.

Gabe pulled bills from his wallet and handed them to the pert blond cashier at the Sailfish Café, then chanced another look at Sarah Ann. She stood among the fishnets and colored glass floats decorating the front entrance of the tiny eatery located just half a block from the hospital, and every line of her body bespoke both impatience and bubbling ire.

She hadn't wanted to have a meal with him, not after their flaming argument, so, perverse bastard that he was, Gabe had insisted. Not that she'd done more than poke at a salad. Not that she'd spared him a single word or glance more than was necessary the entire time.

Well, what did you expect, dogface? Gabe could almost hear Beulah's harsh cackle of derision. Not only had he insulted Sarah Ann with his unwanted attentions, but then he'd added irreparable injury by wounding her feminine pride.

Gabe cursed himself for his clumsiness. He wasn't like Mike, who could always sweet-talk a woman, who always knew which soft words would bring her around to the side of masculine reasonableness. Forget that he was simply trying to do the right thing, to protect Sarah Ann from impulses she would surely regret sooner rather than later.

Despite a chemistry that left him hard and wanting, Gabe knew he wouldn't be good for her, could never be what a decent, loving lady like Sarah Ann needed or deserved. But in being honest, he'd brought down the wrath of a woman scorned on his head, and it was his own damn fault.

The cashier counted his change into his palm as a group
of customers in business attire entered the café. A tall man
in a white, short-sleeve dress shirt and Eton tie fell behind
as his companions went toward a meeting room in the back.
With the instincts of long training, Gabe knew the instant
Sarah Ann stiffened in recognition.

"Sarah Ann." The man appeared trendy in wire-rimmed
glasses and thinning brown hair layered for stylishness. His
pleasant features were grave with concern. Gabe disliked
him immediately.

"Douglas." She straightened her shoulders. "Hello.
Lion's Club meeting tonight?"

"No, County Economic Development Board."

"Any luck bringing in new industry?"

"Some." Douglas flicked a look at the gold band on her
left hand. "So it's true, then."

She clenched her fingers. "Ah, yes."

His expression was as sorrowful as a whipped puppy's.
"I couldn't believe it when I heard—"

But Gabe had already heard enough. Pocketing his
change, he went to Sarah Ann, draping a proprietary arm
over her shoulders and ignoring her startled look. "Ready
to go, darlin'?"

"Uh—" Gathering herself with an effort, Sarah Ann
introduced them. "This is Douglas Ritchie, of Ritchie Real
Estate. Douglas, this is Gabe Thornton, my—" she barely
managed to get the word out "—husband."

Noting Douglas's swift assessment and distasteful dismissal of his rather scruffy attire, Gabe made his response
purposefully overhearty as he offered his hand. "Good to
know you, Ritchie. Any friend of Sarah Ann's, as they
say."

"Mr. Thornton." Douglas wrung hands only for as long
as propriety demanded, and his answering smile was thin.

"I suppose congratulations are in order, though you'll excuse me if I have mixed feelings about the man who stole my girl."

Gabe glanced sharply at Sarah Ann, who blushed and then paled. "I'm afraid I don't understand."

Douglas's colorless eyes flickered behind his glasses. "Sarah Ann didn't tell you about us? Of course, your acquaintance has been so short—what's everyone been calling it? A whirlwind courtship?—that I'm not surprised."

Sarah Ann winced. "Douglas, please. Let me explain."

"Yes, why don't you?" Gabe said, his tone dangerous.

"You see," Douglas began, "I thought Sarah Ann and I had an understanding."

Gabe felt more than saw Sarah Ann shake her head in denial. Deliberately he toyed with the curls springing at the nape of her neck, keeping his tone mild. "Evidently you thought wrong, Ritchie."

Douglas scowled and turned an accusing gaze at Sarah Ann. "Evidently."

Distress etched her features. "Douglas, I'm sorry if—if all this has taken you by surprise, and Gramps and I certainly appreciate your great kindness in offering to buy the farm, but I never encouraged you to believe there could be anything more than friendship between us."

Douglas inclined his head, his mouth drawn into a disapproving moue. "Forgive me if after the time we spent together I dared hope for more."

Pompous jerk. Gabe's irritation mounted. Who the hell did this guy think he was? It took a helluva nerve to chastise a *wife* like this in her own husband's presence!

"Don't blame Sarah Ann, partner." Gabe made his Texas drawl as thick as syrup. "I rushed the little filly right off her feet, didn't I, darlin'?"

Sarah Ann shot Gabe a look that flared with resentment and tried to shrug free of his touch, but he held her firm, fondling her neck, stroking her skin, clearly staking his claim.

"'Course," Gabe continued, "I guess that just goes to show when a man knows what he wants, it doesn't pay to sit around on his . . . uh, laurels too long."

"Gabe!" Sarah Ann chided helplessly.

Douglas's cheeks turned ruddy, and his mouth compressed in an ugly line. "As you say, Mr. Thornton."

"No hard feelings, partner." It was a credit to Gabe's years of training and self-discipline that the genial clap he gave Douglas's shoulder was no more than that. "Best man won, and all that."

Douglas ignored him. "Sarah Ann, I just want you to know that if there's ever any way I can help you, I'm at your disposal."

"Thank you, Douglas," she murmured.

"Mighty nice of you, partner, but Sarah Ann won't be needing any real estate bought or sold now that I'm around." Gabe allowed his mouth to form a lazy grin even though his molars were grinding. He placed a guiding hand in the small of Sarah Ann's back. "Come on, darlin'. We need to mosey on over to the hospital. See ya around, Ritchie."

When they reached the sidewalk outside the café, it was nearly dark, the steamy air just beginning to cool.

"Did you have to be so obnoxious?" Sarah Ann hissed. Her pace down the sidewalk toward the hospital was near world record.

Gabe ambled behind. "Whoa, there, darlin', what's the hurry?"

She turned on him, eyes flashing violet sparks, fists clenched. "And you can cut all that phony cowboy garbage, too! I've never been so embarrassed."

"Yeah, I can imagine seeing that loser on a regular basis would be pretty mortifying."

"How dare you criticize Douglas! He's been a good friend."

"I can see what a saint he is." At the hospital entrance, Gabe held open the heavy glass door, then followed Sarah Ann down the corridor toward Harlan's room. "So why didn't you mention you had this boyfriend waiting in the wings?"

"He's not my boyfriend!"

"He'd sure like to be." Gabe didn't know why the thought set his teeth on edge. "So why didn't you get old Douglas to play husband for you? It would have saved us both a helluva lot of trouble."

"I knew he'd read more into it than I wanted."

"Yeah, he comes across as the pushy type, all right. So tell me, did he ever get you in the sack?"

She went crimson with outrage and embarrassment. "None of your damn business!"

Gabe laughed. "Thought not. He probably requires detailed instructions. Maybe a map or two. Too boring for a hot little filly like you."

She choked. "I'll thank you not to speculate about things that don't concern you."

"Hey, just venturing an opinion." He shrugged, grinning, taking gleeful delight in goading her. "Speaking from my own experience, that is."

"A gentleman wouldn't mention it."

The hospital corridor was crowded with evening visitors and nurses giving out meals and medications. Gabe stepped closer to Sarah Ann's shoulder and spoke into her ear. "In case you haven't noticed, I'm no gentleman."

Then it happened. Mt. Vesuvius blew. The tigress pounced. The star exploded.

Rounding on him with a feline snarl of rage, Sarah Ann shoved the heel of her hand against his solar plexus and slammed him against the wall.

"That does it! You're fired!"

Six

"What do you mean—fired?"

Sarah Ann glared at Gabe, the blood pounding so furiously in her temples she could hardly hear her own voice. "You heard me. Fired. Terminated. I'm not putting up with any more of your antics. Consider this your verbal pink slip! You're officially out of the husband business."

He rubbed the center of his chest, his look sardonic. "Aren't you forgetting a little matter of a license and a ceremony that says differently?"

"How could I forget anything so absolutely abhorrent to me?" With a glance down the busy hallway, she lowered her voice to an enraged whisper. "I feel sick just thinking about it! But at least it's a technicality that can be fixed, thank God. Not like your congenitally perverse and depraved nature!"

"Depraved?" Color stained his tanned cheekbones. "That's pretty harsh."

"It's not half of what you deserve to be called! You've got the delicacy of a bull elephant in heat, and I'm tired of being pawed and belittled out of some sort of sick desire to entertain yourself at my expense."

"Now, hold on!"

"No, it's patently obvious we can't tolerate each other long enough to perpetuate this charade a moment more, so consider yourself off the hook, paid in full, every obligation discharged. Go away. I don't want or need you anymore."

"It's late in the game to be changing the rules." He gestured at the hospital room door. "What are you going to tell Harlan if I suddenly bow out?"

"I'll think of something! You had to take a job flying to Mars, for all I care."

"Another lie." His mouth twisted. "How easy they've become for you."

Hot color rose up her neck, tinted her cheeks with scarlet. "At least Gramps is happy, and without you in the picture I might find some peace to face what's coming."

His expression sobered at this reminder of the seriousness of Harlan's condition. "Despite what you think, I'm fond of the old man. I'll see this through, for his sake."

Dismay tightened her chest, and frustration cascaded through her, the torrent of emotion making her feel incapable of dealing for another second with Gabe's confusing, compelling, maddening magnetism or her own unpredictable impulses and secret yearnings. "Haven't you been listening? I want you gone!"

"And I'm not accustomed to letting other people call the shots for me."

"You'll get over it."

"Not in this lifetime." He took her arm, half dragging her to the door. "Come on, Harlan's waiting."

"Just for you to say goodbye, do you understand?" she snapped. "Then go back to Angel's Landing or Texas or wherever the hell washed-up soldiers go and just disappear. The job's over. You're off the time clock—permanently."

Shaking off his hand, she stormed into Harlan's room, coming up short with Gabe on her heels when she found the head nurse, Lillian, and a graying and slightly paunchy Dr. Stephens bent over Harlan's bed. Alarm jangled down her spine.

"What is it?" she asked. "What's happened?"

"Take it easy, girlie." Harlan's bright blue gaze focused on the nurse working on his arm. "Ouch, Lil!"

"Just a bit more," she said, pulling at a scrap of paper tape. Then, with a smile of satisfaction, she slipped the IV needle free of Harlan's arm. "All done."

"That's better, isn't it, Harlan?" the doctor asked, his manner pleased.

"You're derned right." Chuckling, Harlan waved his arm as Lillian tidied up, discarding tubing and bandages, pushing the IV pole out of the way. "Looka here, girlie. You, too, Gabe. Free at last!"

Totally consternated, Sarah Ann stared, her mouth hanging open, trying to comprehend what she was seeing. "Gramps, what's going on?"

He beamed at her. "Didn't want to get your hopes up, girlie. That's why we didn't tell you."

"Tell me what?"

"Amazing news," Dr. Stephens said, shaking his head. He riffled through Harlan's thick patient chart, flipping pages, pursing his lips as he studied the papers. "The lab work is nearly all back to normal. If I was a man who believed in miracles—and I am—I'd say we've got us a class-A, bona fide one right here."

"What?" Sarah Ann caught her breath, disbelief making way for stunned joy. "You're better? How? Why?"

"The Lord knows." Harlan shook his wispy head in wonder. "Maybe it's seeing you settled with a good man like Gabe, there. Maybe it was that bossy nurse telling me to get well every time I turned around. And maybe I'm just plain tired of lying in this hospital bed all day!"

"Well, you keep up this progress and build your strength a bit," Dr. Stephens said jovially, "and in a few days we'll spring you from this joint."

"Home? You're coming home? Oh, Gramps!" Light-headed and tearful, Sarah Ann hugged her grandfather. Though he still felt frail in her arms, his answering squeeze was reassuringly strong.

"Now, now, girlie." Harlan patted her back awkwardly, and his voice was suspiciously thick. "I'm going to be all right."

Tremulous, overwhelmed, Sarah Ann turned dizzily, and somehow she was in Gabe's arms. She blinked up at him through a sheen of happy tears. "Gabriel, did you hear? I can't believe it."

"Yes, I heard, sweetheart. Way to fight the good fight, old-timer." Gabe grinned at the older man. "Said you were a champ."

"They say it takes one to know one, son, and I knew you were going to be good for the family the first time I laid eyes on you." Harlan looked approvingly at the couple before him and gave a tremendous sigh of satisfaction. "Can't wait to see you two lovebirds at home. Makes joyful an old man's heart, it does."

"At home?" Sarah Ann repeated stupidly. Oh, no! She stiffened in stupefied realization, then jumped when Gabe squeezed her waist in silent warning.

Harlan's eyes twinkled, and his grin sported a leprechaun's mischief. "Heck, next thing you know, I'll be bouncing a great-grandchild on my knee! I can't wait!"

Sarah Ann's face flamed, and Dr. Stephens and Lillian joined in Harlan's indulgent laughter. A devilish light burned in Gabe's tawny eyes.

"Well, darlin'," he murmured, "looks like I'm back on the payroll."

For Gabe and Sarah Ann, Harlan's homecoming five days later was cause for both celebration and dismay. Celebration, because the old man appeared on the road to full recovery. Dismay, because once again, the deception that had begun as an act of kindness had to be played out to the fullest, or that recovery could be placed at severe risk.

Actually, Gabe thought, it had been quite a pleasure to watch Sarah Ann eat crow the day she'd tried to "fire" him. She'd been chagrined to have to ask him to continue the role of husband, at least until Harlan was home and stable enough to accept a "separation." When Gabe acquiesced to her request, he'd been amused at her begrudging gratitude.

Yes, he'd taken a perverse pleasure in watching her squirm, then relented. The only problem now was that when he'd agreed to move into the Dempsey place for a limited engagement as the besotted bridegroom, he hadn't known he'd be relegated to a stint in purgatory on a too-short couch.

Sarah Ann had settled her grandfather into bed a half hour earlier, handed Gabe a stack of linens, then disappeared into her own bedroom. The house was quiet now, the only light streaming from a small fixture in the bathroom. Dressed in a pair of ragged fleece gym shorts, Gabe shivered as the air-conditioning blew a cooling draft across his bare chest and legs. With an annoyed sigh, he punched his pillow, shifted his cramped legs and wondered for the thousandth time how he'd gotten himself into this.

Of course, if he were honest, he had to admit he could have extricated himself from this situation at several different points. Why he hadn't when he'd had the opportunity had less to do with the chords of sympathy he felt for Harlan than with proving a point to Harlan's granddaughter. He wasn't sure what it was about the lady that stirred him up, made him itch to shake her to her very foundations. Maybe he wanted to teach her a lesson about the costs of falsehoods. Perhaps it was a primal male need to challenge her uncertainties about her own womanly attractions. And maybe it was the necessity to prove to her that her low opinion of him was completely warranted.

"What you doing out here in the dark, son?"

Harlan's querulous question jerked Gabe from his reverie. He came to his feet, hurrying to where the old man stood swaying slightly in the hallway, clad in pajamas and robe. He placed a steadying hand to Harlan's elbow. "Uh, just doing some thinking while...er, Sarah Ann gets ready for bed. Something the matter, Harlan? Anything I can get you?"

"Naw, call of nature, is all." With a wave, Harlan shuffled toward the bathroom.

To the sound of water flushing, Gabe hurriedly stuffed his pillow and blanket out of sight behind the sofa. He snapped on a table lamp and picked up an orange grower's magazine. Neither he nor Sarah Ann had really taken into account the logistics of pulling off this charade in such close quarters—other than hanging a few of Gabe's things in her closet and finding room for his razor on the bathroom shelf—but it wouldn't do to upset Harlan with suspicions his first night home. Gabe was reading the magazine, the picture of innocence, when Harlan emerged from the bath.

"Don't keep that lady of yours waiting too long, son," Harlan advised, heading back to his room. "G'night."

"I won't. Good night. Glad you're home, sir."

"Me, too."

Gabe drew a sigh of relief and retrieved his pillow as the door closed behind Harlan. He'd have to make certain that he was up before the old man arose in the morning or the whole scheme was likely to blow wide open.

Gabe hadn't been dozing more than three-quarters of an hour when the rattling of Harlan's doorknob sent him into red alert again. Half-awake, he vaulted toward the kitchen, grabbing up a glass off the cabinet as if he'd just gone in search of a drink.

"You still up?" Harlan queried as he came out of the bathroom again.

"Just on my way to bed now, sir," Gabe assured him. "Anything I can do?"

"Damn weak kidneys. It's hell to get old. Your turn'll come."

Gabe couldn't repress a grin. "Yes, sir."

"You go on to bed now. Don't let the sun set on anger, son. That's good advice for newlyweds."

"Yes, sir. Thanks."

It wasn't the third or even the fourth time Gabe had to make a mad dash for cover that did it, but when Harlan's doorknob rattled again and again in the middle of the night, Gabe finally gave a groan of pure sleepy frustration and gave up. Snatching up his bedclothes, he headed for the only sure sanctuary he could think of. Moving quiet-footed as a cat down the hall, he entered Sarah Ann's room, closing the door behind him the instant before Harlan appeared again.

Covers rustled. With a gasp, Sarah Ann came up on an elbow and turned on the bedside lamp, illuminating a spare and tidy room softened by only a few Victorian pillows, picture frames and a collection of antique perfume bottles on a mirrored dresser tray. Her violet eyes widened when she saw Gabe. "What are you doing? Get out!"

Crossing the small, carpeted room in a stride, he placed one knee beside her hip on the rose-strewn bedspread and clamped his fingers over her lips. "Shh. Harlan's up. Again."

She peeled his hand away from her mouth with her fingers, her look alarmed. "Is he all right?"

Admiring the enticing picture she made in a ruffled white batiste nightshirt, her dark hair flowing in ripples down her back, her skin sleep flushed, he kept his answer low. "Fine, just wearing a rut in the floor to the bathroom. I'm the one who's going psychotic from sleep deprivation. Move over. I'm bunking with you."

She drew a sharp breath and snatched the covers modestly to her chest. "You most certainly are not!"

"Look, the couch won't work with Harlan traipsing back and forth. You want him to realize we aren't really sleeping together?"

"No, but—oh, this is ridiculous!"

He tossed his pillow down on the bed. "Believe me, you have nothing to fear. I've got a full day tomorrow, and I'm too tired to fool around. So relax."

"Yeah, right." Her expression was skeptical. "Don't think I'm going to buy that line of bull, Gabe Thornton. You can sleep on the floor." Rising, she began pushing bedspread and pillows into a pile next to the bed. "Isn't 'roughing it' what you macho soldier types are trained for?"

"Hey, I'm retired, remember?" Enjoying her agitation, he flopped down on the bed. "Not bad. Kinda comfy, in fact. Join me?"

"Not on your life, buster." She scowled at him and snatched her pillow. "I'll take the floor."

"Suit yourself. Can you turn off that light?"

She hit the switch and plunged the room back into darkness, settling down on the floor pallet with an ill-tempered flounce that made Gabe smile. He rolled onto his stomach, inhaling the scent of her that lingered on the sheets, something floral mixed with the unique musk of female skin. His smile died, and he stifled a groan as his body leapt in involuntary response, his desire to bedevil her backfiring. Drawing a deep breath, he willed his recalcitrant libido into compliance.

It was a long time coming.

In fact, sometime in the pitch-blackness before dawn, Gabe decided he would have gotten more rest dodging Harlan's numerous bathroom visits, and the tossing and turning from the floor indicated Sarah Ann was having the same difficulty. When she finally dropped into a restless sleep, only to cry out in troubled dream-muttering, Gabe decided to damn the consequences and lifted her into the bed beside him.

To his surprise she gave a sigh, curled on her side and settled immediately into trusting slumber. Smiling in the darkness, Gabe knew there'd be hell to pay in the morning, but lying beside her felt good, right somehow, the sexual overtones tempered by warm feelings of protectiveness and simple caring, so that when sleep overtook him, too, he felt an unforeseen satisfaction and contentment.

The reckoning came sooner than expected, however. A knock on the door just as the first fingers of dawn crept through the lacy curtains roused Gabe in more ways than one.

"Sarah Ann?" Harlan called through the door. The doorknob turned. "You kids up in there?"

Sometime in the night, they'd gotten tangled up, the attraction of warm bodies melding spoon fashion, Gabe's front curving around Sarah Ann's bottom, his palm pressed against her flat stomach. She came awake with a start, then gasped, both at the position she found herself in and the blatant proof of Gabe's virility pressed against her backside. She tried to get up, but Gabe jerked her back, pressing his lips into the springy curls at her temple with a barely audible groan.

"For God's sake, don't move," he gritted.

Harlan burst through the door, carrying two mugs of steaming coffee and looking quite pleased with himself. "Rise and shine, sleepyheads."

"Gramps." Sarah Ann's voice was hoarse, and a peachy flush flooded her skin as she tugged sheets to her chin. "You shouldn't have."

Looking a bit puzzled, Harlan set the mugs down on the bedside table. "I always bring you your morning coffee, girlie."

"But you shouldn't be up…waiting on us." Her words took on a strangled quality as, unable to resist, Gabe tickled her ankle with his big toe. "You're supposed to be recuperating."

"Pshaw. I feel fine. Best to get back into a routine. Lots to do to get things caught up around this place."

"Ah, it's mighty thoughtful of you, Harlan." Gabe propped on one elbow, giving Harlan a look over Sarah Ann's shoulder, man-to-man and unmistakable in its message. "We'll bring the cups when we finish."

"Huh? Oh, sure." With a nod of approval, he backed out the way he came, barely hiding a grin as he pulled the door shut again.

"Let me go, you snake!" Sarah Ann rolled free of Gabe's embrace. Her hair was a tumbled, seductive mass, and her slender form all shadows and feminine enticement beneath the soft, sheer cotton of her nightshirt. It was all Gabe could do not to haul her back to the mattress.

"Sweet heaven." He blew out a tortured breath and looked to the ceiling for strength. "We've got to get a lock on that door."

"Yes, to keep you out!" she hissed. "How dare you take advantage of me in my sleep!"

Gabe cocked an eyebrow at her, then decided the better part of valor was to lie through his teeth. "Take it easy. You're the one who crawled up here to cuddle with me, don't you remember? Something about a bad dream."

That choked her tirade off in mid-sentence. "I—? No!"

"If I weren't such a saintly kind of guy..." He shrugged, letting her imagine the rest.

Sarah Ann pressed a shaky hand to her lips. "You are no saint!"

"Lucky for you, wouldn't you say, or else I'd never have agreed to your sinful scheme in the first place." He swung his legs to the side of the bed. "What's your complaint? We just gave your grandfather proof positive that the marriage is real. Isn't that what you wanted?"

She speared him with a furious look. "Yes, but you're enjoying this too damn much!"

"Look, sweetheart, there haven't been many perks with this assignment." Rising, he wrapped one fist in her curls, letting the back of his knuckles brush the tip of her breast and evoking her startled gasp. "Be glad I'll settle for a bed and . . ."

Trepidation made her whisper. "And what?"

"Breakfast, of course." He gave a wolfish grin and re-leased her. "Now, are you going to scramble the eggs or shall I?"

A week later, as Sarah Ann worked over yet another skillet of bacon and eggs, she knew she could handle breakfast with the best of them—it was the "bed" part of Gabe's perks that had her befuddled and bemused and as jittery as a cat on hot coals.

In the small farmhouse, with no other options and Harlan's eagle eye ever watchful, she and Gabe were forced to share her bedroom to perpetuate the fiction. So every night she took the pallet on the floor, and every morning, she woke up in Gabe's arms. Thankfully, so far he'd been the perfect gentleman about her climbing into bed with him. She was mystified by her involuntary tendencies, embarrassed that no matter how determined she was to remain at a respectable distance, her subconscious betrayed her.

Sometimes she awakened to find her cheek pressed against his bare chest, his heart thundering beneath her ear. Other times she opened her eyes to find them face-to-face across their pillows, allowing her the momentary pleasure of admiring the length of his sandy lashes and the texture of his morning-stubbled skin before she stole away. Still other times she woke to find herself alone, the sheets still warm from his body, her sleepy mind filled with the fleeting and altogether ludicrous impression that an angel had kissed her as she slept.

Sarah Ann lifted a strip of bacon out of the pan and drained it on a paper towel. At the kitchen table, Harlan and Gabe shared the morning paper over coffee and discussed the day's agenda.

"Got to get that old sprayer serviced before we fumigate the groves," Harlan said.

Gabe nodded. "Rafe knows a mechanic down Port Charlotte way who'll treat you right."

"Good idea. Of course, Tony's got things so stacked up with empty diesel drums and such we'll have to clean that tractor shed out from top to bottom just to reach it. Still, there's a lot of equipment in there we haven't been using like we ought."

"I'll see to it after today's run. I've got to pick up some specimen samples from those biologists at Big Cypress and drop them off in Ft. Myers."

"Maybe tomorrow we can check the inventory. That old tractor needs a good going-over, too."

The men continued their discussion of vehicles and machinery as Sarah Ann cracked eggs into the skillet. While Harlan's convalescence was progressing, his energy levels were not yet on a pace with his enthusiasm, and she was grateful that Gabe continued to pitch in and help around the farm as his own flight schedule and duties at Angel's Landing allowed. It was truly amazing what an extra pair of willing hands could accomplish.

"Two eggs this morning, Gramps?" she asked, popping bread into the toaster.

"Just one, girlie. You trying to make me fat?"

"You need your strength."

"I'm fine. Feed that man of yours."

"Gabe?" She motioned with the loaded plate, then slid it into place on the table at his nod. Catching the collar of her crisp cotton shirt, he pulled her down for a quick peck on the lips—strictly for Harlan's benefit, she knew.

In fact, over the past days, Gabe hadn't missed an opportunity for an overtly affectionate slap and tickle, nuzzle, cuddle or kiss. Just another way to have fun at her expense under the guise of keeping up appearances for Harlan, and a practice that had Sarah Ann wound up tighter than the proverbial eight-day clock.

"Thanks, darlin'." He smiled at her blush and jerked his chin at Harlan. "Beauty and she cooks, too. What more could a man desire?"

Harlan chuckled and raised his coffee cup in a salute as Gabe dug into his meal with a healthy man's appetite.

All in all it was a domestic morning scene straight out of *Blondie*, peaceful, loving, happy—and while it struck chords of yearning within Sarah Ann's secret heart—interior notes that resonated with thoughts of family, husband, children, hearth and home—she knew that it was utterly false and ephemeral. And only a fool would dream otherwise.

Her only defense against her mounting tension was a breakneck pace of her own, a filling of every moment with a manic amount of work. In the past days she'd accomplished more in the way of deliveries, bookkeeping, interviews with itinerant labor contractors and general farm chores with Tony than she had in a normal month's time. The pace she'd set herself was grueling, but exhaustion was a better alternative than having too much time to think and to wish that somehow all this could be real.

"Is that all you're eating?" Harlan eyed Sarah Ann's piece of toast with patent skepticism. "You're going to dry up and blow away."

"I'm not very hungry this morning." The toast tasted like cardboard, so she washed it down with a swig of coffee, then flipped through the stack of mail waiting on the edge of the counter. An envelope from the bank caught her eye, and she slipped it from the pile and opened it.

"Oh, no." The lingering flavor of coffee turned bitter on her tongue with disappointment.

"What is it, girlie?"

"The loan board isn't going to approve what we need to replant the groves." Dismayed, she bit her lip, scanning the letter. "They want to talk about the rest of it, too."

"Those scalawags!" Harlan slammed his fist on the table. "And we've done business with them thirty years."

"It's got to be some kind of misunderstanding, that's all," Sarah Ann said.

Her mind scurried with frantic possibilities and options. She'd been counting on the bank's financing. What would they do now? And Gramps was still in no condition yet to have this kind of concern foisted upon him.

She forced a smile and gave Harlan a reassuring pat on the back. "Don't worry, I'll get it straightened out, just as soon as I rework the figures on next season's tomatoes and get the papers over to Floyd at the packing house."

"No, you won't. Floyd can wait. It all can." Harlan crossed his arms over this thin chest. "Gabe, she's killing herself again with all this work and taking care of me and you."

Gabe pushed his empty plate aside. "I've noticed."

"And are you going to stand for that?" Harlan demanded.

"I don't know. She's pretty headstrong. What do you suggest?"

Sarah Ann huffed indignantly. "I wish you wouldn't talk about me as if I'm not here!"

"I suggest, no I *insist* that you get her out of here today," Harlan said. "She needs a break for her own good."

Faintly alarmed, she shook her head. A whole day spent in Gabe's company? Didn't she have enough problems? "I've got too many things to do—"

"Exactly my point." Harlan gave Gabe a pointed look.

Chuckling, Gabe rose and took Sarah Ann's arm. "Come on, sweetheart, you can't win this one. Besides, haven't I been helping out around here all week? I could use an extra pair of hands balancing those turtle eggs or snail shells or whatever the hell they're sending in today."

Sarah Ann didn't want to appear ungrateful or small-minded, but before she could open her mouth to formulate another argument, Harlan assured her he'd call Judge Hart to come by for a visit and Gabe whisked her out of the door.

By late that afternoon, however, Sarah Ann was ready to admit that she'd been wrong to be overly anxious about the day's trip. In fact, she'd found herself relaxing for the first time in months.

She'd been fascinated by a glimpse into Gabe's professional life, boarding his ebony helicopter at the Lostman's Island airport, watching him pilot the elegant little craft with such absolute control and aplomb that she never had a chance to feel nervous at all. Rather, she felt adventurous, wearing headphones and sunglasses that matched his, and listening to his running commentary about the Big Cypress Preserve and its wildlife over the radio link.

They'd lunched with the pair of biologists camped out in the preserve, and Sarah Ann had been impressed with Gabe's easy manner and the way he'd included her in the conversation. She'd spent an enthralled hour learning about the life cycle of Florida tree snails and endangered American crocodiles, then discussed the state's diminishing watershed and the impact less irrigation would have on struggling tomato farmers like the Dempseys.

After dropping off the scientists' samples in Ft. Myers and returning to Lostman's Island, Sarah Ann admitted that not only had she needed the break, but that she'd had fun. And with Gabe Thornton, who'd been pleasant and entertaining all day long. Would wonders never cease?

"I enjoyed myself today," she told him, rather diffidently, as they drove in his Jeep toward home. "Thank you."

"You sound surprised." He kept his attention focused on the highway, and behind his sunglasses, his expression was inscrutable.

"Maybe I am." She looked at him through her lashes, smiling slightly. "Considering how we're usually at each other's throats, that is."

Gabe chuckled. "Even leopards change their spots occasionally. Harlan's right, though. You work too hard. You should do more for yourself."

"It wasn't how I was raised."

"Neither was I, but you can get over it." He pointed suddenly. "Mike and Rafe have blazed a trail across that frontage property of yours. Want to see?"

Curious, she nodded. "Sure."

Wrenching the steering wheel, Gabe turned off the highway, jouncing the vehicle along a barely marked path through saw grass and palmetto. "With direct access, Rafe thinks we can rent camping spaces to the snowbirds. He's got a place marked up ahead."

"Seems a good idea." Sarah Ann held on to the door as the Jeep bounced along the uneven track, then splashed through a shallow creekbed, one of the many small tributaries that fed into Paradise Bay. Higher up, under a stand of stunted pines, a bulky figure with startling red hair squatted on a plastic ice chest and dipped a fishing line into the sluggish water. "Look, isn't that Beulah?"

"Sure looks like it." Gabe tooted the Jeep's horn, only to receive an ill-tempered glare and an imperative gesture with the tip of the fishing rod to keep moving.

Sarah Ann laughed. "It doesn't appear as she wants company."

"That battle-ax is pure, antisocial venom through and through. If she weren't such a fine cook..."

"You talk big, but I know you three men couldn't do without her."

"That's what you think," he said, his expression sour. He turned the Jeep into a small thicket of pines. "Besides, she talks to herself."

Sarah Ann smiled. "Lots of folks do that."

"Not like her. Rants and raves, directs full conversations at the sky. Weird, if you ask me. Here we are." He parked the Jeep. "Come on, I'll show you where Rafe laid out those spaces."

Trooping through the tangle of sea grape and salt myrtles, Sarah Ann dutifully admired the layout of the future RV park. Following him back to the vehicle, she had to admit that it would be an innovative use of land that could never have been turned into productive tomato fields. And trading it away for an almost-husband might just have been the thing that turned Gramps around, so she couldn't regret it a moment.

"I know you'll be successful—ow!" Something sharp pierced the thin leather sole of her sandal and stabbed into her heel. She gasped in pain.

"What is it?" Frowning, Gabe took one look at her and scooped her up, carrying her back and plopping her down on the hood of the Jeep. The metal was pleasantly warm through her denim jeans. He peeled off his sunglasses, hooked the stem in the crew neck of his shirt, then began to strip off her footwear. "Let's have a look."

"I don't think it's bad." She bit her lip and shivered, not as much from the pain in her heel as from the feel of his fingers against her sensitive instep.

"Let me see . . ."

She sucked in a pained breath as he probed, then plucked an inch-long thorn from her heel. "Golly."

Gabe produced a first aid kit from inside the Jeep. "Don't faint on me, sweetheart. This is going to sting." Gently, he poured antiseptic on the wound, holding her still as she jerked.

"I'm okay," she said finally. "You didn't have to go to this trouble."

He peeled paper off a sticky bandage and applied it. "We're tropical here. Just like any other jungle, you can't take chances."

She looked at his face. "You must have seen a lot of jungle."

"Enough to know it's a terrible place to die."

That bothered her. Almost without volition, she reached out and touched his knuckles, wanting to offer some comfort. "But these hands are trained to protect, to save lives."

"And to take them," he said harshly. His eyes burned into hers. "Don't romanticize it, ma'am. You should be afraid of me."

"Don't 'ma'am' me, Gabriel." She touched his cheek, stroking the tension in his jaw. "And you protest too much."

He shuddered violently and caught her hand. "Don't!"

Embarrassment flooded her. She'd forgotten herself, forgotten that he'd been subjected to her untoward attentions all too often of late.

"I—I'm sorry," she stammered, blushing and pulling back. "I don't mean to make this more awkward than it's already been. We really need to consult that attorney about the annulment, now that Gramps is better. And I'm sorry about crawling into bed and disturbing you, I don't know why or how I—"

She broke off, frowning, trying to read his expression. He wouldn't meet her eyes. Realization hit her with the force of a sledgehammer. He was guilty. Guilty as sin.

"Wait a minute...you lying, thieving snake! You've been the one all along!"

"Now, Sarah, how can you accuse me of such a thing?" His voice was mild, but his eyes were full of devilment, and she knew she wasn't mistaken. He'd let her think . . .

"Aughh!" Enraged, she shoved him hard.

The movement made her slide off the slick metal hood and land right between Gabe's thighs. Gabe's hard, muscled thighs, and the bulging manhood lovingly cupped by faded denim. Something powerful changed behind his eyes, and he bent his head to hers, muttering.

"Oh, hell, now you've done it."

Seven

Gabe's mouth on hers, hard, compelling. The taste of masculine need on his tongue. Sarah Ann's anger burned, flared, in an instant changed, consumed her with white-hot lust.

Hands that intended to reject, reached instead. Lips that meant to let fall words of harsh condemnation, nipped and tantalized in silent demand. Repudiation became acceptance; denial, hungry consent.

His response was as immediate, as volatile. Crushing her to him, he groaned into her mouth, the evidence of his burgeoning need pressed intimately against the throbbing juncture of her thighs. He leaned her against the sun-warmed hood of the Jeep, exploring the sweet cavern of her mouth, stroking her tongue with his until she shuddered with the pure carnality of it. Behind her closed lids, the sun burned golden haloes, and that's how he felt to her, heated as the sun, beautiful and golden and tawny.

Impatiently he unbuttoned her shirt, pushed aside the cotton knit of her simple bra and cupped the lush heaviness of her breast. When his thumb flicked the pebbled nub, she gasped and nearly levitated, surging against him in overwhelming hunger, sliding her hands under his T-shirt, letting her palms glide, reveling in the soft bramble of hair over hard masculine muscles. When her fingers scraped the washboard of his stomach, then slipped beneath the low-slung waistband of his jeans, he uttered a guttural growl.

Releasing her mouth, he lifted her swelling breast, then caught her nipple between his lips, suckling strongly. She cried out, clutching his head between her hands. A ribbon of sensation unfurled between that rose of sensitive flesh and the kernel of feminine desire between her legs.

Threading her fingers through the raw silk of his hair, she hesitated when she discovered a ridge of tissue hidden on his scalp, mute evidence of the risks he'd taken, the wounds he'd suffered, and her heart overflowed. Pressing her lips to the top of his bent head, she curved her leg around his calf, straining for the ultimate closeness.

It was primitive, primal. It was male and female, the ancient instinct to mate reduced to its basic element.

Gabe transferred his attentions to her other nipple, laving the tip into a tight pearl, feasting in voluptuous gluttony. She whimpered, clutching at his shoulders, then found the curl of his ear with her tongue. He went wild.

Sliding his hands down to cup her bottom, he lifted her onto the hood, pressing her backward, opening her jeans and kissing the damp tangle at the apex of her thighs through the thin cotton of her panties. She gasped, but the molten languor of passion infused her blood, and she had no choice but to surrender to its power. Decadent and unrestrained, her breasts bared to the sun and the most secret part of her to his questing mouth, she lay like a pagan sacrifice, opening herself to the timeless ritual.

He pursued her through the rite, relentless, taking her higher and higher toward the pinnacle with his lips and fingertips, allowing no quarter, no retreat, until she writhed in exquisite agony. Her skin bathed in moisture, her hands twisted in his hair, she arched upward, giving, taking, lost in delight. When the throbbing tension became unbearable, when fiery sensation filled every cell of her being to the brim and she knew that no human could endure such glory and live, he released her with a final skillful flick of his tongue and flung her over the edge of the world.

Stunned, she cried out, pleasure radiating from her core in convulsive waves. Even then, he wasn't satisfied, urging her into another flight before she once touched the earth, shattering her universe into shimmering shards of wonder. Limp, dazed by the powerful ripples of passion, she opened her eyes and found him looming above her, blocking the sun. A predator's intentness made his expression hard, but his eyes burned golden with male dominion, male pride.

She couldn't let him get away with that.

Crooking her elbow around his neck, she drew him down to her, kissing him voraciously, tasting her own erotic essence on his lips. Lifting her legs around his hips, she pulled him even closer. Reaching for him, she found the hard ridge of male flesh beneath the soft denim and fondled him boldly. He jerked, went rigid, then ground himself against her hand with a groan. Control destroyed, he thrust once, twice, to completion, then collapsed on top of her with a shudder, gasping, his lips pressed against the salty curve of her neck. Closing her eyes, she smiled with female pride, female dominion.

After an eternity, when the world stopped quaking, reality intruded. The unyielding metal hood against her back.

The soft sucking noise of damp flesh leaving damp flesh as Gabe levered himself away from her. Regret in his golden eyes.

Sobered, chagrined, she slid to her feet, fumbling with her clothing, looking anywhere on earth but at Gabe. How the hell did that happen? Oh God, what now?

"Don't beat yourself up."

Her head snapped around, sending her curls flying about her flushed face. The salty air was suddenly so muggy she felt suffocated. "What?"

"We've been living in each other's laps, sleeping in the same bed." He sawed a hand through his hair. "An explosion was inevitable."

"What a convenient excuse," she murmured.

Her condemnation could have been directed solely at him, and yet she knew that wasn't the truth. No, she was horrified at her own weakness and susceptibility. She hadn't had the strength to resist, indeed, had welcomed his passion unequivocally, uncaring of the falsity and complications it could only bring. What kind of woman did that make her?

Gabe grimaced, and for such a big man his attitude was strangely helpless. "Sarah—"

"No. I don't want to discuss it." She climbed into the Jeep and stared straight ahead, her tone leaden. "Just take me home."

Sarah Ann was eternally grateful when Gabe muttered something about business at Angel's Landing and said he'd be gone for the evening. Facing him over the supper table after what had passed between them was more than she could have endured.

Slicing another tomato, she arranged it on top of the chef's salads she was preparing, something cool and easy and all she felt capable of at the moment. Gramps napped on the living room sofa, tired out from a day's "jawing" with Judge Holt. She was grateful that he'd been too fatigued to ask more than a desultory question or two about her outing with Gabe. She couldn't face that, either.

In fact, she felt so confused and unsettled, she didn't want to confront anything. But that was the coward's way, and no matter how she wished it were different, she could no longer avoid looking the situation squarely in the eye. She was in big trouble.

The phone pealed, and she grabbed it quickly to avoid waking Harlan. "Hello?"

"Sarah Ann, it's Douglas. How're you doing?"

In her muddled state of mind, Douglas's soothing, undemandingly friendly voice was a welcome balm, so welcome that her own words wobbled slightly. "Fine, just fine. It's good to hear from you. After last time—"

"Nothing can change my regard for you, Sarah Ann."

She smiled. He might be a bit pompous, but her battered ego sopped up his syrup like a dry pancake. "I value your friendship, too, Douglas."

"Well, it's as a friend that I'm calling. I came across a piece of news today at the Development Board that's sure to concern you."

Something in the gravity of his tone made alarm bells go off in her head. "Oh?"

"I have it on good authority that it's in the works to raise property assessments substantially—and soon."

"Oh, no." Her thoughts clicked over at a frantic pace. First the bank, now this!

"It'll put everyone in a pinch, but the bigwigs are determined to push it through. Going to fund some new industry developments, or some such nonsense. Will you be able to handle it?"

"I don't know," she said truthfully, rubbing the bridge of her nose. "And certainly not if anything else happens.... Everything's such a struggle right now."

"Look, I know it's not what you want, but my offer is still open. I'll give you a fair price for the place, and you and Harlan can retire."

"I—I can't think like that, Douglas. This is our home. All I ever wanted was to keep the Dempsey legacy intact."

A peevish irritation colored his retort. "Then why'd you deed over that piece of land to Gabe Thornton?"

The question startled her. "It was a ... a wedding present. He and his partners want to make improvements at Angel's Landing."

He was immediately placating. "I'm sorry. I didn't mean to question you, it's just that I'm worried about you, Sarah Ann. I can hear that something's not right. 'Marry in haste, repent in leisure,' as they say. Maybe you're having second thoughts?"

Her defensive hackles rose. "That's none of your concern."

"I know, I know, but I do care a great deal about you. I want you to know, whatever happens, I'm here to help you in any way that I can."

"I appreciate that, Douglas." She sighed. "And thank you for the offer, but I'm sure Gramps and I will hang on somehow. We always have."

Disappointment clipped his words. "If you're certain, I won't bother you again. Just remember that I'll always be here for you if you need me."

"Yes, thank you. You're a good friend."

She said goodbye and hung up, chewing her lip. Douglas was a friend, and a generous one. Perhaps she'd underestimated him. If only she'd gone to him instead of Gabe....

Shaking her head, she put futile regrets out of her mind. She couldn't second-guess her actions at this point. She had to deal with the situation as it was now.

It was addictive to live in the same house with a man like Gabe. She'd been fantasizing, pretending on a certain level like some sad old maid that it was all real, and that was unfair to both of them. She blushed in every cell of her being to think how far things had already gotten out of hand, and with her own behavior so abandoned and wanton, it was just a matter of time before they'd go too far entirely. Unquestioningly, she had to prevent that at all costs, give them both back their freedom before it was too late.

Crumbling bacon on top of the salads, she added a dollop of ranch dressing and made her decision. Gramps continued to improve, so the threat of his having a relapse at bad news was ameliorated each day, especially if that bad news was couched in the gentlest terms. It was time to bring this piece of fiction to an end. She'd tell Gabe tonight that their "marriage" was over and he had to leave—her home, her life, her mind—for good.

Simple. Straightforward. Businesslike.

Placing two salad bowls on the table, she went to wake Harlan, knowing that she wouldn't be able to eat a bite, knowing that nothing in this life was ever as easy as it sounded.

"What you doing out here all alone, dogface?"

"Don't bother me, Beulah."

Stretched out in his favorite hammock, Gabe stared up at the starlit sky and ignored the gargantuan form standing in the shadows, the tip of her ever-present cigarette glowing orange in the midnight darkness.

"Feeling guilty, huh?"

Yes, ma'am, because I can't keep my damn hands off her! And she deserves better....

"Go away."

She gave a caustic chuckle. "Must have been a helluva brawl."

"None of your damn business."

"Sorry for yourself, too?" she hooted. "How the mighty do fall!"

He ground his teeth. "Anybody ever tell you you're a royal pain in the—"

"Lots of times. Obedience ain't my strong suit. Kinda like you."

"I know my duty."

"Oh, yeah?" The raspy voice was full of mockery and skepticism. "Hear tell something about a vow, 'cleave only unto her.' What you got to say about that one?"

Gabe sat up with a savage curse. "Leave me alone, damn you."

"You ain't no yellow-belly, are you, Gabriel?"

"Don't play your mind games with me."

"Let me tell you something, rookie, that little girl needs you just as much as you need her."

"Like a hole in the head, you mean."

"She's scared, too."

"Dammit, Beulah, shut up!" He surged to his feet, ready for combat, but his tormentor had vanished, disappearing into the thick greenery without so much as a whisper to mark her passage. "Beulah?"

Frustrated, he kicked the base of the palm tree, his teeth clenched on a flurry of curses. Damned busybody! Always poking her long nose where it didn't belong. He'd a mind to kick her out on her wide fanny and dare Mike and Rafe to question him. What the hell did she know, anyway?

Gabe jammed his fists into his jeans pockets and threw his head back to the night sky, breathing in the salt-flavored air in great gusts, striving for calm. An impossibility, since all he could think about was Sarah Ann, her taste, her passion, her hurt.

Damn, how could he have treated her like that, used her for his own pleasure with no thought to her feelings? There wasn't a man lower on the face of the earth than Gabe Thornton. No matter what the situation with Harlan, Gabe knew he had to get out of Sarah Ann's life—*now*—before he did any more damage.

First thing in the morning...

A fist clenched inside Gabe's chest. Nebulous uneasiness rose like a bubble under pressure and popped on the surface of his consciousness.

Scared. Beulah said that Sarah Ann was scared. And, of course, he'd made her feel that way on more than one occasion. It was only natural...

No, that wasn't right. Gabe shook his head, frowning. There was something else. Apprehension skittered up his spine like a spider, unnamed, unfocused, a presentiment of imminent disaster. Only one other time in his life had he felt anything like it, when life and death had warred in a jungle of fire and destruction, and that experience had taken his heart, left him scarred and devastated.

He struggled with the irrationality of it, fighting for a logical explanation while his instincts shrieked. He saw a pair of wide violet eyes. He felt her fear, could taste its metallic essence on his tongue. A litany beat in his brain.

Too late. To her. Too late.

"Sarah!"

And then he ran.

He hadn't come home.

In the dark, silent house, Sarah Ann sat curled in the big

easy chair, huddling under her thin seersucker robe as if to ward off a winter's chill. It was silly to feel rejected when her own resolve had been to end the—what?—affair, relationship, business deal? Still, her feelings swelled inside her chest to overwhelming proportions, and a tear slipped from the corner of her eye.

She'd jumped at every strange sound for the last hour, thinking it was finally him. Every distant panther scream, every crunch of gravel, every whisper of breeze in the live oaks brought her heart to a thunderous cadence. And each time, when no lights shone in the drive, no Jeep wheeled up before the house to park in Gabe's accustomed place, the letdown left her limp and demoralized.

He could at least call, she thought, then stifled a wild laugh. How like the wronged wife that sounded! And she had no right to even think such a thing. She had no claim on Gabe Thornton. Never had. Never would.

Restless, preoccupied, she rose and wandered into the kitchen, wiping at the dampness on her face. She couldn't even force herself to go on to bed. There were already too many memories in the room they'd shared.

A night bird's shrill cry drifted through the open window over the sink, momentarily quieting the loud chirring of cicadas. Sarah Ann leaned her elbows on the sink's edge and closed her eyes, letting the sultry air caress her skin, her thoughts tumbling.

This is how it's going to be when he's gone. It's what you want. Get used to it.

Pain and piercing loss stabbed her, and she inhaled sharply. An acrid aroma tickled her nose, scalded her tongue. Her eyes flew open. Smoke!

Barefooted, she rushed to the back door, threw it open. An ominous flickering glow lit up the equipment shed.

"Oh my God!"
And then she ran.

Gabe knew it was going to be bad even before he saw the flames.

Dread clogged his throat like the thick smoke that drifted over the Dempsey place, an invisible but suffocating pall in the darkness. The Jeep was still rolling when his feet hit the ground.

"Sarah Ann!" Bursting through the front door, he realized in a flood of relief that it wasn't the house.

"What the devil—?" A light flicked on, and Harlan stood in the doorway of his room, blinking like an owl.

"Fire. Call the fire department." Barking the order, Gabe pushed opened Sarah Ann's bedroom door. Nothing. Panic slammed into him like a giant fist. "Where is she?"

But he already knew, with a certainty that twisted his gut. And then he was out the door, running.

A macabre, pumpkin-colored light danced around the tractor shed, tossing sinister shadows against the night. Crackling, spitting, the greedy enemy within the structure licked at wooden tomato crates, paper boxes of labels and twine, bottles of chemicals, fuel that ignited with a sudden whoosh of air, leapfrogging blazes toward empty diesel drums and a lineup of still and silent machinery. Rising heat buckled the tin roof, made it wail and groan like a living thing.

The hair on the back of Gabe's neck stood at attention at the agonized sound. Buried memories stirred in their graves, gruesome images of another place and time. The dank jungle, a warehouse with more sinister purposes, a simple hit-and-run mission to save the world. Failure. Paralysis. Death.

A flicker of movement caught Gabe's eye, brought his mind back to the present and his heart to his throat. "Sarah!"

He charged into the shed, hands raised to protect his face from the surging temperatures. Against the distant wall, determination written in every inch of her, a small feminine figure in a flimsy robe unbelievably dragged a dribbling green water hose toward a wall of flames threatening a green and yellow tractor. Then she vanished behind a puff of ebony smoke.

"No!" His roar of protest sailed upward and was lost amid the fire's banshee howls.

Not failure again. Not this way, God. Not Sarah!

Flames scorched his face and singed the hair on his arms. Hot death seared his lungs. Heedless, he plunged through the choking veil, searching blind, frantic in his helplessness and despair.

It was happening again. People depended on him, and he let them down. In the distant recesses of his memories, weapons chattered and the dying screamed. Smoke and flames, disaster and destruction. And he should have perished, too, and he would have, except for—

For an instant, the smoke parted, the light changed, shimmered with an ivory glow, like the inside of a translucent pearl. Wondering, he knew he'd seen—or sensed—it before, if only he could remember, and he reached out to touch it.

And found Sarah Ann.

"Gabe, thank God!" Gasping, coughing, her face streaked with tears and soot, she struggled with the hose. "The tractor—help me!"

The alabaster curtain dropped, and he was again in the world of black shadows and crimson flames and choking air and the reality of danger. He grabbed her arm.

"Forget it! We've got to get out of here!"

"No, we can save it. I—"

Instincts, training, divine communication—something electrified Gabe and he flung them forward. With a shriek, the smoldering wooden rafters above them shifted, gave way, crashed at their heels. Running, dodging bursts of flame, he dragged her unerringly through the thick clouds of smoke, out the shed entrance, into the sultry summer night.

Incoherent, crying, she struggled against his hold, beating at him with her fist. "The equipment—save something—we'll be ruined! Let me go!"

"Sarah, stop—"

A fireball went up behind them, knocked them off their feet, landed them scraped and bruised and breathless in a heap in the middle of the grassy backyard. Gabe scooped Sarah Ann against his bulk, covering her with his body, protecting her head with his arms as debris rained down. In the distance a siren wailed.

When Gabe lifted his head, the shed was totally involved, a monster conflagration of orange and scarlet flames and black skeleton melting into oblivion over the carcasses of incinerated machinery. Sarah Ann pressed a trembling hand to his chest. He shifted his weight, and she sucked in a deep breath, her eyes wide and dazed as she stared up into his face.

"Are you hurt?" he asked, his words smoke roughened.

"I—no, I don't think so. What happened?"

"Fuel tank must have exploded." He levered them to a seated position, his expression going savage. He refrained from shaking her senseless by only the most superhuman effort. "You're a madwoman, you know that? Trying to do it all by yourself, as usual. What the hell's the matter with you? You could have been killed!"

"So could you!"

"Oh hell, not me." With a gust of bitter laughter, he climbed to his feet and dragged her up beside him. "Never me. I've got some evil genie who watches my back and won't let me die. It's more fun to see me suffer."

Shadows flickered across her startled features. "What do you mean?"

He bared his teeth in a snarl. "That I was lucky this time, and no one else died because of me."

"Gabe, what is it?" She rubbed his shoulder, her tone soothing. "We're okay. That's all that counts. You're absolutely right. I was very foolish, and you were wonderfully brave. You found me."

He passed a hand over his eyes. "Thank God the light changed. White, just for a second. Did you see it?"

Bewildered, she shook her head. "No. Gabe—"

A shiver danced up his spine, and he clamped his lips together to still the sudden chattering of his teeth. "Never mind."

"Hey, you two kids okay?" Harlan shuffled across the grass toward them just as the Lostman's Island Volunteer Fire Department arrived in a pumper truck, followed by a pickup carrying Gabe's partners.

It was a reminder that the night's work was far from over. And sometimes it didn't pay to ask too many questions. Ignoring Sarah Ann's wide and worried gaze, relegating imponderables to another venue, Gabe stepped forward to take charge.

The shed and everything in it was a total loss. By dawn only a smoldering pile of melted metal and ashes remained. The fire department packed up their hoses and left. Mike and Rafe finished a firebreak to contain any lingering sparks, ate the substantial breakfast Sarah Ann fixed for all of them, then went home, too. Harlan went to bed with a mild sleeping pill prescribed by Dr. Stephens. And then it was just Gabe and Sarah Ann, begrimed, fatigued, numb.

"I ran you a hot tub." She carried antiseptic and clean towels to the kitchen sink. "Let me clean those scrapes before you get in."

"I'm all right."

She'd given her face a perfunctory wash and replaced her dingy, singed robe with an oversize knit shirt and shorts. She looked as innocent as a little girl, but it was the woman who sighed. "I'm beyond arguing with you, Gabriel. Please."

Shrugging, he went to the sink and stripped off his ruined shirt, letting her sponge the raw places on his elbows and forearms. He eyed a newly scabbed abrasion on the back of her arm. "You could use some attention yourself."

"Maybe we'll trade places if you behave. Careful, this will sting." Biting her lip, she doused his wounds with antiseptic, wincing when he sucked in a sharp breath. "Sorry."

"No problem." He stuck his hands under the faucet and splashed his face, then blotted with a towel. "Your turn."

She held stoically still as he cleaned her arm.

"I'm sorry we couldn't save anything," he said, dabbing at the scrape. "But with insurance..."

"There wasn't any." She pursed her lips, whether against the tenderness of her arm or the pain of the financial loss, he couldn't be sure. "And Douglas told me today that property assessments are going up. Together, it may finish us."

"God, Sarah Ann, I'm sorry."

"There are more important things in life, I guess." Turning, she looked up at him, her violet eyes questioning, fathomless. "What did you mean earlier? About dying?"

He looked away. "Nothing. Shock makes a guy babble."

"Damn you," she said, her words soft as a caress. "We both could have died. Tell me the truth. This has happened to you before, hasn't it? I have to know."

Gabe's lips twisted. Yeah, she needed to know. So that she could recognize him for what he was and truly despise him. Maybe that would be a kindness, after all, a way of helping her put this whole tawdry episode and Gabe Thornton behind her.

So he told her, in the most brutal terms, and watched her lovely face go white.

He told her about leading a team into a jungle stronghold, the mistakes in judgment and command they'd made. His responsibility, how the mission was jeopardized in the blink of an eye. Devices they'd planted to put a stop to the manufacture and distribution of a vicious new chemical had turned the place into an inferno, but Rangers never left their dead behind. Oh, he'd been there, in the thick of it. When the shell had split his scalp to the bone, he'd known his own time had come, only there'd come a light, compelling and leading him, and unquestioningly he'd followed, coming out of the dark tunnel intact while six good men perished.

And afterward, the suspension, the inquiry, the hard questions. He'd eventually been exonerated and reinstated. Hell, they'd pinned a damned medal on him! For shutting down an operation that would have taken thousands of innocent lives, the commendation had said, but all the time Gabe knew...

"Knew what?" Her question was gentle as an angel's kiss.

"That I should have died with them."

"And those who came out with you? How many?"

"Thirteen."

"Captain, can't you count?"

His face turned to stone. "It's more than numbers, don't you understand? They were my men."

"All soldiers know the risks. You'd lost men before." It wasn't a question.

"Not like this." Turning away, he bowed his head and gripped the edge of the sink. "Some demon possessed me, a demon called cowardice, I guess. I—I don't remember much. A face, the light . . . carrying Mike."

"Mike? You brought him out on your back, I suppose."

"That's what they said. It's pretty much a blur."

"And since you can't see through that blur, you think you're guilty of some heinous crime?" Her voice rose, indignant with mounting fury. "What monumental ego. What colossal nerve!"

He straightened. "You don't understand."

Infuriated, she punched him in the chest. "I understand plenty. You'd rather wallow in self-pity and guilt than deal with genuine human emotions, because that might be too hard. You'd rather deny the miracle of your own survival, because to acknowledge it might mean you should do something with your sorry life!"

Gabe caught her shoulders. "Woman, you go too far!"

Moisture welled in her eyes, turning them the color of rain-drenched pansies. "A man can't be weak, so you'll never admit we've meant something to each other these past weeks, either."

"Sarah, don't."

"Needing someone isn't weakness, Gabriel." Gently she placed her palm over his heart, stroking the place she'd so recently abused. Her voice was honey sweet, whiskey rough. "It's strength."

Her tenderness undid him, and he reached for her, groaning a desperate prayer. "Then God forgive me, I've got to have you."

Eight

He tasted of smoke and unshed tears.

Wrapped in Gabe's arms, possessed by the magic of his mouth, Sarah Ann inhaled his grief, the secret vulnerability of a man of iron. She put all of her heart, all of her tenderness into her response, the offer of succor and sweet surcease for a man who'd never allowed himself to hope or dream of such treasures, never thought himself worthy of such riches. And when he trembled and pulled her closer, she knew then that she loved him and had from the first.

As a revelation, it should have been devastating, yet the acknowledgment liberated her, left her feeling light as a wisp of cloud. Understanding replaced confusion. From their first meeting, everything about him had called out to her, and because of circumstances, she'd denied her own instincts. It was the headiest freedom to follow her heart, to give in to the impulses that surged through her blood and made her feel truly alive. It was the grandest, most sobering moment of her life to be the one who touched this man, and, God willing, made him whole.

Nothing else mattered. Nothing else counted.

Straining on tiptoe, she clasped her arms around Gabe's strong neck, plying the soft sun-streaked hair at his nape, stroking the scar that marked his pain, letting her fingers say what words could not. His tongue was in her mouth, hot and potent, and she met each tantalizing thrust of exploration with a parry of her own, matching stroke for stroke his growing excitement, his blossoming need.

Awed by his force of will and sheer physicality, she'd been attracted initially by his masculine strength, everything feminine in her yearning to melt into his hard muscularity, but now she was the powerful one. When he lifted his head to give them breath, she moved her mouth down his breastbone, licking at his salty skin like a voracious kitten, pressing him back against the edge of the sink. She felt him stiffen and smiled to herself, then scored his flat male nipple with her teeth and heard him groan.

Gabe caught the back of her neck, threading his fingers into her dark curls to steady himself. She was relentless, lapping at his bronzed skin, teasing the indentation of his navel with her tongue, pressing kisses to his ribs. Sliding her hands around his waist, she delved beneath his waistband and found the shallow hollows at the tops of his hips, scooping them with her fingertips, delighting in her own daring and audacity.

Something low and dangerous rumbled in his throat, a predator's warning that she was pushing too far, too fast, too boldly. Laughing softly, she tossed caution to the compass points, daring him to resist with a renewed onslaught of lips and hands and feverish caresses.

Rising to her unspoken challenge, he reclaimed the lead. Clasping her face between his palms, Gabe took her mouth once more, drinking of her sweetness like a man finding a sparkling oasis after an eternity of desert and desolation. Gladly she gave to him, joy bubbling within her like a crystal fountain.

His lips were warm and rich, his taste as intoxicating as fine wine. Light-headed, dizzy, she clung to him, leaning into the V of his legs, fully aware of the rigid bulge that revealed his need. He traced the curve of her spine with his fingers, then dragged the oversize shirt over her head and cupped her naked breasts.

In the pale dawn light, the sight of his big, tanned hands against her creamy flesh was an erotic rush. Sarah Ann watched him through her lashes and shuddered with the sheer wanton pleasure of it. Her skin felt too tight, steeped in sensation, every nerve singing for more, and he gave it to her, gently plucking at her distended nipples with his nails, lifting the heaviness of her breast in his palm, stroking the velvety underside until her knees were jelly and her core liquified.

"Beautiful." Tawny eyes hooded, he breathed the word like a benediction.

And she felt it, accepted it, knew that in his eyes she was lovely and desirable and all things feminine. A sense of wholeness, of rightness, filled her being and made her glad to be here and now with this special, this soul-wounded, this perfectly human man.

Covering his hand with her own, she felt the tensile strength in his fingers, the subtle tremor that told her he was not unmoved. His cheekbones held a high color; his night-stubbled jaw a curious tension, as a wild thing caught unawares by a taming hand. Lips curving, she smiled at him tenderly, every molecule of her longing to give him solace and comfort and passion.

"Come with me," she said.

Startled, he looked up, his expression wary. Threading her fingers in his, she drew him down the hall and into the modest, white-tiled bath, shutting the door behind them. The single-bulbed fixture over the sink cast shadows across the stacks of navy and yellow towels, the tumbler that held their toothbrushes, the confusion on Gabe's lean features.

"Sarah, what—?"

"Shh." She murmured against his lips, her hands busy at the snap of his jeans. "The water's still hot."

He jerked in surprise, and his eyes narrowed. "That's not all."

She laughed. "Just get in."

"Yes, ma'am." Kicking off his boots, he drew a sharp breath as she helped push his filthy jeans down his hips.

Sarah Ann caught her own breath at the sight of him fully aroused. Magnificently naked, he climbed into the tub and sank down in the steaming liquid. His bent knees made islands in the bathwater, and he relaxed his arms on the tub ledge, his eyes never leaving her flushed face. Heart pounding with anticipation, she swallowed hard, then knelt beside the tub.

Lathering her hands with a bar of spicy bath soap, she rubbed the suds across Gabe's chest and shoulders, neck and back, attending him like a mythic houri. His lashes fluttered, and his head fell back against the tile. A low rumble of pleasure vibrated in his throat.

Sarah Ann was in the grip of just as powerful and mesmerizing an experience. A tactile delight of the first order, the slick, soapy bubbles glided against hard flesh; the scent of soap and steam tickled her nostrils. With the supersensitivity of the blind, her fingertips tingled, swirling magic across his burnished hide, finding the subtle and seductive nuances of masculine bone and muscle. She couldn't get enough, wanted to absorb him through her skin, striving to know and learn him through an erotic and mystical osmosis.

Lifting a hand, Gabe idly brushed the backs of his knuckles against her breast. The rosy crest puckered, budded, became hard and pebbled, and Sarah Ann gulped for air. Shivering, she rubbed the pads of her thumbs through the white suds, circling his male nipples, then scraped her nails through the wet, curling bramble of hair on his chest.

Gabe's skin rippled under her ministrations, and he drew a gust of air between his bared teeth. Feeling bold and courageous, she slipped her hands beneath the lapping water and touched him intimately, her fingertips exploring the blatant proof of his arousal, steel encased in velvet.

It was too much. Like a cougar pouncing, Gabe caught her hand. His voice was a raspy growl of warning. "You're asking for trouble."

Provocative as Eve, she smiled. "Yes, please."

"Lady, you got it."

With a swiftness that took her breath, he dragged her over the edge of the tub, sloshing sudsy water onto the tiles in giant waves. Pulling her on top of him, he captured her mouth in a drugging kiss, his hands working at the waistband of her drenched shorts.

She helped him, wiggling until she was free of the binding garment, sighing at the ultimate delight of being finally pressed next to him, limb to limb, with nothing between them but a film of lather. Cramped and tangled within the confines of the tub, all that mattered was to touch and be touched. She lay between his legs, the hard ridge of him against her belly, her arms looped around his neck. He feasted on her mouth over and over again, until she was dizzy and dazed.

Sweeping his wide palms over her, he tested the textures of every sensitive spot—the softness under her arm, the flare of her slender hips, the curve of her knee, the tender folds between her legs. Sarah Ann moaned, straining closer.

Wet skin, cooling water, heated mouths. Fiery sensation overloaded nerve endings. They broke apart, lungs bellowing, fighting for oxygen. Gabe lifted her away, bending his head to take her nipple into his mouth, sipping the water from her sensitive flesh, driving her inexorably toward the brink of madness.

When she thought she couldn't endure it a moment longer, he shifted again, turning her so that her back was to his chest. Stroking her breasts, her belly, even lower, he whispered hoarse love words into her ear. She clasped her fingers around his strong wrists, holding on to him as the world dissolved around her like the last lingering soap bubbles floating on the tepid water.

An empty ache consumed her center, a place only Gabe could fill. She arched against him, restless, showing him her need, and he answered her, spreading her thighs, lifting her from behind in the buoyant water, the tip of his manhood probing intimately. She shuddered with want. Giving, loving, she leaned back against him and opened herself, gasping at the sheer bliss of it, and slowly took him inside her body.

"Sweet heaven." Gabe groaned against her ear, his breath feverish. One hand splayed low on her belly below the water, holding her still, his fingertips delving into the soft thatch at the top of her thighs.

Panting, her head lolled back on Gabe's broad shoulder, her eyes closed, Sarah Ann savored the sensation of being one with the man she loved. He held her with exquisite tenderness and possessiveness. She had never felt so protected, so safe, and yet perched on the brink of incredible excitement and imminent discovery. With this man, she could experience it all.

She whispered his name in wonder at the miracle. "Gabriel."

He took her sigh as a signal and began to move, slowly, fractionally, with scrupulous care. The water shimmered with tiny ripples, lapped about their legs. He grazed down the curve of her neck, kisses that made her skin quiver and her blood rush. The tempo he set was slow, unhurried; his movements gentle, yet definite, taking them both toward the inevitable resolution.

"Oh, what you do to me," he said, his breath gusting in her ear. "You can have anything you want."

Moving with him, meeting the increasing intensity of his thrusts with a full measure of eagerness, she moaned softly. "You. I want you."

"Ah, Sarah, ma'am, you already have me."

His husky words made her wild, but when she bucked against him, he held her back, building the anticipation with delay, guiding them with his strength of will as passion escalated, letting the rapture mount slowly, by subtle increments. Teased and tormented, golden honey poured through her veins, sweet and warm and exotic.

But then the tension was too much for him, too, and he lost his place, the rhythmic pace faltering, growing erratic. His loss of control thrilled Sarah Ann, and she swirled her hips, evoking Gabe's gasping curse of pleasure. In sweet retaliation, he slipped his fingers lower, stroking the throbbing bud of sensation. She cried out, shuddering as completion overcame her, falling, falling into a maelstrom of shining light and blinding satisfaction.

It seemed to go on and on, waves of delight spilling from her very core, radiating to every nerve, filling her heart. Gabe held her as she rode the crashing breakers to completion, but then her rhythmic inner contractions gripped him, and with a groan he sailed into paradise at her side.

Still a part of his body, Sarah Ann lay cradled in his arms, limp and exhausted, yet utterly at peace. The air cooled her damp skin. The water was cold, the tub uncomfortably cramped, but she was too content to move. Gabe's unsteady breathing wafted past her ear, drifted in warm gusts across her breasts. Her nipples contracted, and the most secret part of her—the part that Gabe still claimed—quivered in shocking response.

His arms circled her, and his words were husky with a need that matched Sarah Ann's own. "It's not enough."

"No."

With a strength that amazed her, he shifted them apart, then stood with her in his arms, water sluicing from their skin. His eyes burned. "Then we'll find out what is."

They'd shared her bed, but never like this.

Daylight filtered through the bedroom curtains, spilling lacy, filigreed shadows across Sarah Ann's alabaster skin. Her eyes were the purple of thunderheads, dark violet and mysterious and watchful. Sprawled naked together on the rose-strewn sheets, Gabe admired the beautiful and erotic picture she made, amazed and humbled at the liberties she'd allowed, the utter giving and openness that let her lie quiescent and unperturbed under his perusal after hours of heated exploration and explosive pleasure.

It was a gift he didn't deserve.

It was a mistake he shouldn't repeat.

And God help him, at this moment, nothing mattered a damn but holding her again.

With regret, he noticed the swollen outline of her well-kissed mouth, the rosy abrasions from his beard that marred her silken skin at jawline, neck, breasts. He ran a fingertip over a reddish mark on the upper swell of her bosom.

"I hurt you. I'm sorry."

She smiled, sultry and tousled and desirable. "It was worth it."

His loins tightened. This woman worked a magic on him that was incredible in its intensity, in the sheer power of it to stir him with a mere look, a single word. He drew a breath. "When you say things like that you destroy my good intentions."

That pleased her. "Good. You've been hidebound too long. You have to be free to heal."

He gave an uneasy chuckle. "What is this, a rescue mission?"

"Maybe someone already did that."

Sandy brows lowered in a frown. "Meaning?"

"The light you saw. Twice it's happened, you said. Don't you wonder—?"

"No." He threaded his hands through her springy curls, loving the vibrant feel, and kissed her gently. "No. I took a lick on the head the first time, then had a flash of déjà vu, that's all. Forget it."

"Why must there always be a logical explanation?" Her gaze was tender. "There are more things in heaven and earth than mere mortals can know, Gabriel. You must be special indeed to warrant such attention."

"And you're being fanciful."

"Am I?" She brushed his hair back from his forehead. "You are a singular individual, Gabe Thornton. Kind, honorable, worthy of happiness. Why do you find that so hard to accept?"

His mouth twisted, and he shrugged. "Out of practice, I guess."

"Then let me prove it to you."

Pulling his head down, she kissed him, running the tip of her tongue against the seam of his lips in silent entreaty.

Without thought, he deepened the kiss, sipping of her essence like nectar. Her hand splayed on his hip, satin and fire coursing from her touch, bringing him to instantaneous hardness, resurrecting need in a flash of burning light.

But it was too fast, and he knew he'd hurt her, so he tried to hold back. Her fingers closed over him, gloving his heated length, wringing a groan of purest pleasure and agony from his throat.

"No, Gabriel. *Now.*"

He couldn't deny her. He couldn't deny himself.

Rising above her, holding himself on his hands, he positioned himself, then plunged into her silken depths. And knew he'd never felt anything so good. Her eyes widened and she gasped, clasping his buttocks, welcoming him, tugging him closer still.

How can it just keep getting better? he asked himself, gazing with wonder down into her beautiful, love-flushed countenance.

She was warmth and liquid honey, so tight and hot he feared he'd go off like a green boy at the slightest movement, yet he couldn't stop himself, lifting almost free, then gliding home with a powerful thrust that made her gasp again. Gathering his control, he paused, looking at the place were they joined, male to female, knowing he'd never seen anything so beautiful as the two of them together.

It was a glimpse of heaven, probably the closest he'd ever come to a blessed hereafter, and all the more poignant to see it and know he couldn't hope to hold such a treasure, could only take this moment in time and make of it what he could.

"I never want to forget this." He moved again, grimacing with the exquisite pleasure of their joining. "I never will."

She rose to meet him, giving him everything, her gener-osity and passion flowing like a wellspring of forgiveness and redemption. "Gabriel, love me."

Her husky plea destroyed him, and he abandoned con-trol, plunging into her, lost and broken and fearing in his soul that here was his only salvation. But then thought was beyond him, and sensation ruled. Taking her mouth, he kissed her with longing and terror. She clung to him and they moved together, striving, searching, the pounding tempo of desire driving them to a completion more pow-erful than they'd yet experienced.

Sarah Ann stiffened beneath him, her cry of ecstasy muffled against his lips, her limbs quivering in release and something more. Gabe inhaled the sound, felt her flesh close around his body, and exploded, shuddering and shattered as the universe flew apart into a million shining pieces.

But the only piece of the cosmos he cared about was the woman in his arms. In that moment, when he held his wife tight and they floated in that vast, uncharted space be-tween heaven and earth, an outrageous idea stunned him.

Selfish bastard that he was, maybe he could find a way to keep her.

Sarah Ann lay in the crook of Gabe's arm, listening to him breathe as he slept. The angle of the sun through her bedroom curtains told her it was almost noon, but the house was still, only the whir of the air-conditioning breaking the silence. The stench of smoke hung heavily on the air even here inside the house, a grim reminder of Dempsey loss.

But the reality of financial ruin was nothing compared to the utter devastation in Sarah Ann's soul.

Oh God, what have I done?

Her body ached in strange and unusual places, mute evidence of passion requited. But the ache in her heart was much more painful, for to love a man she couldn't have was an unforgivable mistake of judgment, a selfish blunder of monumental proportions, an error from which, having now fully experienced Gabe's tenderness and ardor, she knew she'd never truly recover.

She swallowed hard, fighting the prickle of guilty tears. How she wanted what they'd shared to be real, to be a permanent part of her life! And she'd wanted it so badly, she'd let her heart rule her head, pushing him with her words when he was vulnerable and shaken, then taking the physical surcease he offered, unmindful of consequences.

But there was a price to be paid now, for the annulment was impossible, unless they both were willing to perjure themselves. A bitter grimace twisted her lips. What's another lie at this point?

Gabe's arm lay heavy and relaxed across her waist, and she turned her head to look at him. His fair hair brushed his brow, but even in repose his face was too harsh and masculine to be called boyish. Her fingers itched to stroke the golden stubble gracing his jaw.

Obsessed, that's what she was, and had been from the first. Her heart contracted painfully. She had to accept that loving him gave her no rights, no special claims to his affections, and to hope otherwise was an unreasonable and illogical expectation.

But that might not be the worst of it. Would Gabe think she'd planned a seduction to trap him? Would a misguided sense of integrity make him offer to "do the honorable" and stay now that they'd consummated the marriage? She shuddered. What would be worse than living with a man who despised you for a treacherous liar?

No, a bargain was a bargain, despite hours of ecstasy in each other's arms, and she would make no attempt to hold him, nor would she permit him to stay out of guilt or duty. Thank God she hadn't confessed her love for him, for it would only make what she had to do more difficult.

But for right now, before reality intruded, she could be forgiven if she indulged herself just a little, living the fantasy, lying replete and well-beloved in her husband's arms. She lifted a hand to his slumbering features but didn't touch him. Her lips moved soundlessly in words she longed to say aloud, but didn't dare.

I love you, Gabriel.

At the faint sound of a vehicle coming up the drive, her hand fell away. When minutes later Harlan knocked on the bedroom door, she was outwardly calm, inwardly resigned.

"Gabe, you up?" Harlan bellowed.

Gabe roused, shaking his head groggily and automatically pulling Sarah Ann into the warm curve of his naked body. His lips grazed her bare shoulder, making her shiver uncontrollably. "Yeah, I'm awake."

"Them partners of yours are out here waiting."

"On my way." Still drowsy, he dropped a swift kiss on Sarah Ann's mouth and rolled to his feet, then stopped. "Hell, where's my clothes?"

"Clean things on top of the dresser."

She bunched the pillow under the crook of her arm and pulled the sheet over her breasts, watching him dress—briefs, jeans, shirt. The domesticity of it wrenched at her heart. Another indulgence. But there were few enough left to her, so she memorized each movement, every strong, lean line of his body, to resurrect on a bleaker day.

Gabe tugged the shirt over his head, muttering and rubbing his face. "Hope to hell Harlan's got coffee made. You want a cup?"

"Thank you, no."

"Mike and Rafe offered to help shift some of that debris. No real hope that anything can be salvaged, but you never—"

"Gabe?"

He paused halfway to the door, a sheepish look crossing his face. "Huh? Oh, hell, I'm sorry, sweetheart. I'm out of practice being a sensitive lover. You just catch me up short whenever I—"

"It's not that. I just wanted to tell you that despite—" flushing, she pushed to her elbow and gave a wave that encompassed the rumpled sheets "—all this, I think we should proceed with the annulment or divorce or whatever it takes. And . . . and you should move out right away. Today. I'll explain things to Gramps somehow."

For an instant he looked stunned, then his expression hardened and his eyes went blank and unreadable. "You don't say."

She did her best to keep her tone cool, but her fingers knotted in the sheet. "It's for the best, don't you agree?"

"I don't know. Your decision seems rather precipitous, considering."

She tilted her chin. "I'd already decided to tell you last night before the fire."

"Then why—?" He broke off, his mouth twisting, his gaze dropping insolently to her cleavage. "Maybe you'd like to explain?"

"We all do crazy things under extreme duress." She shrugged. "You, of all people, should understand that."

A mirthless chuckle rumbled from his throat. "Absolutely."

"Then just accept what happened and forget it, okay?" she snapped. Holding the sheet to her bosom, she struggled to a seated position on the side of the bed, her bare feet dangling. "You told me I should do something for myself, and I did. I'm sorry if that distresses you, but we're adults, and at least we both enjoyed it, I guess."

He gave a mocking bow. "Thank you for that."

The heat of a humiliating blush stung her cheeks. "You know as well as I that this is what we'd agreed to do all along. Last night changes nothing."

"As you say, we're adults. But it's hard for this ole Texas boy to shift gears so swiftly, ma'am." Crossing back to her, he caught her chin, forcing her to look into his eyes. "Especially when you're sitting there naked."

She drew a sharp breath.

"Don't get all ladylike and huffy on me now, Sarah. I've had you moaning beneath me, remember? Of course, whether I'm here or at Angel's Landing, and whether we're legally tied or not, now that I've sampled your charms, I'm going to be hard-pressed to just forget all about it." His lips curled in a wicked, mocking grin. "But what the hell, I'll spring for dinner and a movie for the chance of a repeat performance."

Incensed, she slapped his hand away. "Why are you making this so difficult?"

His look turned sardonic, and she regretted the outburst immediately. She couldn't believe he was truly hurt, of course, but no man enjoyed being the first to be rejected. Well, let him lash out at her. She could take it. Coolness was the key. *It's just business.* It wouldn't do to show him how the idea of her never seeing him again made her long to howl with despair. She owed him a modicum of dignity, an ending that left pride intact.

Taking a deep breath, she met his gaze squarely, ignoring the way her heart shriveled inside her chest. "I beg your pardon if I've offended you, Gabriel. I was too blunt, perhaps, but I ask you to respect my wishes in this matter. A clean break will be better for us both."

His jaw worked. "If that's the way you want it, ma'am."

"That's the way it has to be."

The cool civility of their words after the glory of what they'd shared speared icicles through Sarah Ann's heart. Her lip quivered and she bit the inside so hard the salt-sweet taste of blood coated her tongue.

Gabe's features held a stern implacability, and his eyes were flat and mud colored. "Fine. I'll clear out this afternoon."

"Thank you."

He opened his mouth to speak, then closed it again. It had all been said. All except for one thing.

With the swiftness of a swooping eagle, he bent and latched his mouth to hers, spearing the sweet interior with his tongue in a final, breath-stealing possession. Then he released her just as abruptly, leaving her dazed and reeling.

"Damn you," he said softly. Then he walked out of the room, out of her life, pulling the door shut behind him with a sharp click of finality.

Sarah Ann collapsed on the rumpled bed and let the silent tears come.

Nine

"What a mess."

Gabe stood at the edge of the smoldering, sodden ruin that had once been the Dempseys' equipment shed and agreed with Mike Hennesey's assessment. "You can say that again."

The redheaded ex-Ranger shook his head and followed Rafe through the debris as Harlan, haggard from his sleepless night, looked on from a seat in a folding lawn chair. Dressed in heavy boots and jeans, Gabe's partners explored carefully, poking here and there and turning over mysterious clots of incinerated sludge with long-handled shovels. The twisted and warped skeletons of now-unidentifiable machinery littered the blackened, devastated scene, a desolate moonscape of cinders and ashes.

Under the brilliant blue of a noonday sky, the reek of stale smoke stung Gabe's nose, and the taste of ashes lay as bitterly on his tongue as Sarah Ann's repudiation lay on his soul. Toeing a melted scrap of tin aside with his boot, he cursed his own gullibility.

Hell, he thought, he felt as though he'd been sucker punched, and it was his own damned fault. Didn't he know women couldn't be trusted? Even a woman whose loving soothed a man's inner soul, whose generosity and passion stilled the demons inside him. Why had he thought even for a moment that she was any different, just because her touch had almost made a believer out of him again? Especially this woman, who'd invented a lie and then lived it with such cool calculation?

Maybe Beulah was right. Maybe he was a jerk.

Yeah, a jerk to think a decent woman might hook up permanently with the likes of you, Thornton.

At least Sarah Ann had the good sense to realize the folly in that. Despite her sweet words to the contrary, Gabe knew she saw through him, right to his rotten, unworthy core. No wonder she was ready to run like hell. Jaw clenching, he reached for the sunglasses hooked to his crew neck and slipped them on as a defense against his painful thoughts.

What was he griping about, anyway? Their so-called marriage was never supposed to be real. Just because they'd scratched the sexual itch didn't mean the basic plan had changed. He was indulging in a fit of male pique because she'd been the first one to state the obvious, that's all. Hadn't he already made the decision to tell her he'd had enough? She'd simply beaten him to the punch.

He gave a grunt of self-disgust. Grow up, Gabe.

Looking across the horizon at the distant tomato fields, he swallowed hard. Sometimes it was damned difficult to know just how to act when there was a gaping hole in your gut and the emptiness was eating you alive.

Skirting the perimeter of the burnt area, Gabe went over to Harlan, who was gazing at the devastation as though he'd lost his last friend. Gabe clamped a hand to the old man's shoulder. "There's not much to save, if anything."

"Well, son, we did our best, I suppose."

Gabe gave him a sharp look, noting the grayness around his mouth. "You feeling all right, Harlan?"

"Smoke's given me the headache."

"You sure that's all?"

Harlan shrugged, his gnomish countenance bleak. "Just tired of fighting. Sometimes it seems the Lord's just out to get you, you know?"

"Yeah. I know." Gabe squeezed Harlan's shoulder.

What would Sarah Ann's announcement that the "marriage" was over do to her grandfather's recuperation? Over the weeks he'd known Harlan, Gabe had developed a real affection for the crusty old man. Not only that, but the work they'd accomplished on the farm had brought Gabe a sense of satisfaction he hadn't experienced in a long time, maybe since he was a kid in Texas. He'd made an investment in the Dempseys and their ranch, but it was time to let that go, too.

Why did that knowledge provoke a pang of loss? He didn't really belong here, Gabe reminded himself. Besides, he had Angel's Landing and the charter service to keep him busy. His life was full. It was more than enough. It had to be.

And if he swallowed any of that malarkey, he was a damned fool!

Gabe cast a glance toward the house, frowning. When he'd kissed Sarah Ann, he'd meant to prove something, and yet she'd tasted of sweetness and spent desire and a faint coppery tang of blood. Perhaps she wasn't as dispassionate as she would have him believe? A woman couldn't come apart in a man's arms over and over again without feeling something deeper than the purely physical for the man holding her, could she? He snorted at that piece of wishful thinking. It didn't matter, because he knew he didn't have the courage to ask Sarah Ann what she really felt for him or if they might stand a chance together.

Hell, he couldn't even answer those questions himself! He knew she aroused in him emotions that had lain dormant in the chill of a soldier's emotional deep freeze. She provoked all the rages—anger, lust, frustration. She made him so crazy sometimes he wanted to throttle her, but at the same time, one look into those pansy-colored eyes and all he wanted was to make her happy.

And since in his heart of hearts, Gabe knew that he was the last man on earth who could do that job, the best thing was to accede gracefully to her wishes and bow out of her life with as little upheaval as possible. He owed her that much.

"Hey, Cap'n!" Across the field of ashes, Rafe waved to him. "Have a look."

"Be right back, Harlan."

The older man gave a tired grin. "Take your time, son. I'm not going anywhere."

Gabe picked his way across the wreckage. "What you got, Rafe?"

Squatting on his haunches, the wiry Seminole used a stick to lift a small mass of fused metal. "I'd say what you got is serious trouble, Cap'n."

Gabe frowned, recognition and suspicion scalding his brain. He mouthed a curse. "Is that what the hell I think it is?"

Rafe nodded. "Right. Your basic all-purpose incendiary device. Cap'n, this fire was no accident."

"Where the devil have you been?"

At Gabe's savage growl, Sarah Ann came up short in her

bedroom doorway. Features dark with anger, he pitched a bundle of clothing onto the bed and glared at her. His hair was sexily rumpled, and he still looked better than any man had a right to in tight jeans. It just wasn't fair.

Dismay sapped the last of her strength, and she sagged against the door casing, feeling wilted despite the coolness of her scarlet tank top and short denim skirt. She'd waited until well past dark to come home, hoping it would all be over, that he would have packed up and cleared out by now. The hard part behind her, then she could have begun to pick up the pieces. But she was not even going to be granted that small mercy.

"Well?" he demanded.

How could she admit she'd hidden like a coward all afternoon, performing chores that no longer seemed important? When the banks and stores closed and it grew dark, she'd fled to the Stop 'N Go to sit in the back office with Merrilee, drinking diet colas and nibbling broasted chicken and listening to her friend's inconsequential gossip, knowing full well Merrilee suspected something was seriously wrong but had the grace to wait until Sarah Ann was ready to tell her about it. Which she might never be. But her soon-to-be-ex-husband had no right to interrogate her like a war criminal!

She straightened her spine and lifted her chin. "None of your business."

"Damn you, woman!" Catching her arm, he jerked her to him, his golden eyes flaring with temper. "As long as we're still man and wife, what you do with yourself *is* my damn business! Now get that perfect fanny of yours in gear, you're coming with me."

"What are you talking about? I—" She broke off, realizing with a shock that he had been packing *her* things, not his. "Wait a minute! *You're* the one who's supposed to be leaving."

"Yeah, well, things have changed." Scooping up the assorted garments, he stuffed them in one of her old tote bags and hustled her toward the door. "I'll tell you about it on the way."

"Way? Way where?"

"Angel's Landing. Come on."

She tried to dig in her heels, to no avail. He doused the lights and had her across the porch and halfway to his Jeep before she could splutter another protest. "Wait! What about Gramps?"

"Harlan's already gone over there. The smell of smoke gave him a migraine. You two are going to be our guests for a few days."

"You must be out of your mind! I'm not going anywhere!"

"That's where you're wrong, sweetheart." At the Jeep, he paused and gave a low whistle. In the underbrush at the edge of the dark yard, a flashlight blazed on, then off in an answering signal. "Okay," he grunted, "let's go."

Mystified, she stared into the darkness as he stuffed her into the Jeep. "Who was that? What's going on?"

"Rafe's going to take the first watch."

A sudden chill skittered down her spine. As Gabe accelerated down the drive, she licked dry lips and asked carefully, "Why does anyone need to watch my house?"

The lights from the dashboard cast greenish shadows over Gabe's grim expression. "Because someone deliberately set last night's fire, and if the bastard decides to come back, we're going to fry his ass."

Sarah Ann's breath left her in a little whoosh of disbelief. "Deliberate? That's impossible."

"We found evidence. It was arson, all right."

She shook her head. "I don't believe it. Why would anyone do that?"

"You tell me. Got any enemies you haven't mentioned?"

"No! That's ridiculous. It must have been vandals, or kids messing around."

"Kids don't normally use a high-tech timing device and plastic explosive. It was professional."

Sarah Ann felt the blood leave her face. "Oh my God."

"Yeah. That's why I'm not taking any chances. Until we find out what this is all about, I consider it my duty to stash you and Harlan where I can keep an eye on you."

Duty. That he couched his concern only in those terms slashed her heart, and the pain raised her defenses like a porcupine's prickly quills.

"I appreciate your consideration," she said stiffly, "but I'm sure that we can handle it without all this melodrama."

He snorted. "Like hell. I'm involved, whether you like it or not, and any threat to you is something I take very personally. I'm going to get this guy."

She was beginning to feel more desperate, torn between wanting Gabe's help and the need to have their parting behind her. How could she bear to keep going through it over and over again? As it was, the agony of being so close to him again was nearly killing her.

She cleared her throat, endeavoring to keep her tone even. "I'm sure the police—"

"—will be notified in due course." He pulled the Jeep to a stop in front of Angel's Landing. Bands of golden light streamed from the main building, winking and glittering on the dark surface of Paradise Bay like pirate's treasure. "They'll do what they can, which isn't much, so I'm going to poke around on my own first before the trail is disturbed. Since we don't know anything, I didn't see the sense in disturbing Harlan."

"He doesn't know it was arson?"

Gabe came around to open her door, grabbed up her tote bag and took her arm to lead her inside. "We'll tell him when we get a definite lead. For now, as far as he's concerned, he's here simply until the smoke smell clears."

"And me?"

"You'll stay with me until I say you can go."

His high-handedness made her angry, and the thought of their continued cohabitation filled her with dread and alarm and a shameless anticipation. How could she let this happen? When she spoke, her voice shook. "That's not what we agreed this morning."

"That was before I knew some bastard was threatening my woman."

The possessiveness in his voice sapped the force from her automatic protest. "I'm not your woman."

"Say that three times fast while I'm buried inside you and maybe I'll believe you."

Outrage accompanied a surge of primal heat, and she gasped. "You can't do this."

He pushed her through the front door into the well-lit hall, his mouth a flat line. "Yeah? So sue me."

A pair of cardplayers looked up from their hands at Sarah Ann and Gabe's entrance. Under their curious regard, her hiss of defiance died in her throat. With an air of disgusted defeat, Mike threw down his cards. Beulah reached into the pocket of a hot-purple Hawaiian shirt for her cigarettes. She lit one off the stub she held, then blew out a stream of smoke and eyed Sarah Ann critically.

"Gabriel, ain't you got better sense than to keep a tuckered-out woman up to all hours? Some men are selfish jerks, ain't they, honey?"

"I couldn't agree more." Sarah Ann's fervent reply accompanied the glare of dislike she flung at Gabe.

"Lay off, Beulah," Gabe growled. "I've got no taste for your brand of poison tonight. Where's Harlan?"

"In bed, which is where you better put that little gal. She looks all in."

"Yeah, Beulah sent Harlan off to beddy-bye all right," Mike said, grinning. "After she flat cleaned him out at five-card stud."

"Cheating again?" Gabe demanded.

"Of course not." Beulah's black eyes gleamed, but her tone was lofty. "The man was overconfident."

"For God's sake, Beulah!"

Mike burst out laughing. "Take it easy, Cap'n. He had a helluva good time. Got rid of his headache kibitzing with the witch queen here."

Sarah Ann bit her lip. "Maybe I should check on him."

"He's fine," Mike said. "It was mighty entertaining, I can tell you. Said he hadn't had so much fun in years and went off to get a good night's sleep."

Beulah gave a wave toward the rear bungalows. "After all the excitement you've had, you two young'uns better follow suit. Heck of a thing, fires. Stirs up memories. Takes away certainties. Best rest up and count your blessings."

A case of sudden jitters provoked Sarah Ann's protest. "Really, I'm not all that tired."

"Nonsense. Changed the sheets and put some sandwiches in the fridge for you. Now git."

Gabe scowled at the cook. "When are you going to figure out you're not the one giving the orders around here? I never saw a woman as bossy."

Mike's green eyes sparkled with mischief. "That's what Harlan said, too."

Gabe transferred his attention to his partner. "You'll relieve Rafe?"

"Around midnight. Depend on it." Mike nodded. "See you in the morning. Good night, Sarah Ann."

"Good night." Subdued but seething, she had no choice but to let Gabe propel her out the back toward his cottage. The shell path crunched underfoot, underscoring her resentful mutter. "I still don't think all this is necessary...."

He opened the bungalow's door, hit a light switch and pushed her over the threshold into the tidy apartment. "Look, I'm the professional here. Until we know what's really going on, I'm not going to let you take any unnecessary risks. So relax and let me do my job, okay?"

"No, it's not okay." A welter of conflicting emotions and a simmering tension caused by Gabe's nearness beset her. Poised on the plain area rug, ready to take flight like a doe scenting danger, she hugged herself in an effort to contain a wild trembling. "This isn't your problem, and I can take care of myself and Gramps without your help!"

"Yeah, so far you're doing a heck of a job." He flung her tote bag onto the battered leather sofa. "Let's see— tangled up in a phony marriage, trouble at the bank, property assessments doubled, hospital bills to pay, and now you're taking it on the chin with this fire and no insurance. Not to mention the creep that set it is still on the loose. Honey, you may not know it, but you're going under for the third time and there's no rescue ship in sight."

When he laid it all out in a lump, their troubles loomed as tall as Mt. Everest and seemed just as insurmountable. Her voice rose with desperation. "I'll figure something out—downsize, cut production, sell off a piece of the property if I have to."

"You need more help and fresh capital. Look, maybe I could come up with something—"

She gasped. "Don't you dare offer me charity!"

"Damn your stubborn pride, lady," Gabe's jaw worked, and he jammed a hand through his hair in pure irritation. 'Why do you feel you have to do it all by yourself? Didn't you tell me needing someone was strength? Well, you need my help, and I'm here to give it to you."

"For how long?" Her stricken whisper was raw with pain. "Don't you understand? I won't let myself depend on you. It wouldn't be right."

"If I say you can, you can. So don't worry about a minor point of ethics."

His failure to understand cracked the fragile shell of a composure she'd been battling to maintain since he'd walked out of her bedroom earlier that day. Hot tears spurting, she dropped to the sofa and buried her face in her hands, her breath catching on a single anguished sob. 'Can't you see I can't stand any more?"

"Sarah, don't." He squatted in front of her, drawing her fingers away from her wet face, and his voice was gruff and strangely wounded. "I see plenty. I know you can't stand me. After all that's happened, I can understand that you hate my guts. I don't want to hurt you, but dammit, I can't just sit back and do nothing when you're in trouble."

Through a haze of tears, she looked at him in amazement. "Can't stand you? Are you blind? I'm in love with you!"

He drew a hard breath. "God."

"I'm sorry, I never meant this to happen." Moisture slid down her cheeks, and she babbled explanations and excuses. "It's my problem, not yours. You'll have your freedom, I promise, but that's why I told you to go. I can't see you like this, it's too hard—"

"Sarah, darlin'." Leaning forward, he cupped her face, brushing her lips with his.

She moaned in equal parts pain and pleasure. "Oh please, don't do this to me."

"You don't mean that."

She gasped against his mouth, shivering, denial on her lips but acceptance in the hands she slid up his shoulders. "I do. I do mean it."

His tongue sipped the salty essence of her distress from her cheekbone, moved to the tremulous corner of her mouth. "Then send me away."

Ah, he was a devil, tempting her to destruction with his strong hands, his warm lips, his golden eyes, and then taunting her for her weakness.

"God help me," she murmured brokenly, "I can't."

The sound he made deep in his throat was both victory and urgent need. Rising, he pulled her into his arms and slanted his mouth across hers.

She was too weak to fight him, and, although a part of her whispered that she would pay a price for this, she was too needy at that moment to deny herself. When his tongue probed, she parted her lips, welcoming his sensual foray with both sinking fear and utter delight.

Crushing her to him, he shuddered at her response, taking her mouth over and over until she was dizzy and clinging. Slipping fingers beneath the strap of her tank top, he explored the silkiness of her shoulder and the fragrant curve of her neck with his lips. Every nerve strumming, Sara Ann twined her fingers through his hair and pressed herself even closer.

With a low mating growl, Gabe lifted her and carried her into the bedroom. The only illumination was the wide band of light falling from the open doorway across the foot of the bed, leaving the rest of the room as shadowy and mysterious as the hard planes of Gabe's intense countenance.

Laying her gently on the bedspread, he stripped off his shirt and flung it away.

He seemed something out of a dark legend then, burnished and ebony in the dimly lit space, muscular and powerfully male, looming over her like the fallen angel namesake of his past life, but divinity or demon, she didn't know which. Nor did it matter, for she was under his tempter's spell and powerless to resist his sorcery. He reached for the snap on her denim skirt and undressed her slowly, smoothing caresses and heated kisses as he revealed each inch of satiny skin.

Bewitched, she trembled under his touch, gasping as his lips grazed the tips of her breasts, the velvet concavity of her stomach. His hands were man-rough and electrifying on her sensitive skin, stirring her to new heights of arousal.

Restless, she reached for him, needing to share the enchantment, but he would have none of it, capturing her wrists and holding them next to her ears as he plied her mouth with hot, wet kisses that took her breath and what was left of her sanity. Still in his jeans, he sank against her, and the eroticism of her nakedness against his half-clothed state jolted through her like heat lightning, melting her core.

She whimpered with need, thoroughly overwhelmed, controlled and excited by his male hunger, yet trusting implicitly in the genuine gentleness in his soul and the sure knowledge that he'd never harm her. Responding, Gabe shifted his weight and released her hands. His supple, tormenting fingers slid between her legs, stroking her intimately, probing her secret places with heart-stopping expertise, making her gasp and arch against his hand.

He groaned against her mouth. "You're so hot, so wet. Is that for me?"

"Yes." She smoothed her hands over his shoulders, adoring the feel of him, inhaling the unique scent of his male musk, quaking in every fiber of her being with love for him. "Only you. Always."

"Thank God."

Rising, he shucked off his jeans in one swift move and came to her again, arms and legs tangling as he kissed her into oblivion. Rolling to his back, he lifted her so she straddled him, surprising her as he passed control of their passion into her hands. Bending, she pressed her lips to the center of his chest and opened her body for him, letting the slow slide of gravity join them, smiling against his skin in exultation at his deep, pleasured groan.

Her own pleasure was just as intense, and she shuddered uncontrollably, the dark sweep of her hair brushing his face, his neck, his chest in a voluptuous torment. Gabe gripped her buttocks, holding her still for a timeless moment, absorbing the feel of them as one. If the millennium had come at that moment, Sarah Ann would have been content to find eternity in Gabe's embrace. As the need inside her became urgent and she began to move, she did find a part of it, a gift given in time to two lovers.

Gasping at the joy of it, she arched her back, riding the crest of a wave of delight. His face hard with passion, Gabe watched her, touching her breasts, fondling the place where they joined. She felt his tension building and redoubled her efforts, surging against him until his breathing was ragged, pushing him past control or thought with the power of her loving; determined to give him everything that was in her.

He closed his eyes, gritting his teeth, holding on to her as he rose to meet her movements. "Darlin', I can't ... you'd better hurry—"

"Let me," she breathed, a wicked, provocative motion of her hips wrenching another desperate gasp from him. "I want..."

She couldn't finish, for thought had flown and pure sensation ruled, and she could only show him what was in her heart. And he felt it, clasping her in his strong arms, pulling her tight, his massive body shuddering, surging to a thunderous completion. His pleasure became hers, his final thrust the catapult that lifted her into space, plunged her into the fiercest heavenly sun to melt and explode in golden glory.

Afterward, there were no words left to say. Gabe held her in the darkness, his fingers stroking her hair. She lay against his chest, listening to the thump of his heart beneath her ear.

He'd been right, she thought. She was his woman, if not his love. But there was no pride in that, no honor, and certainly no peace. While her body still reverberated with the aftershocks of pleasure, her pain was too deep for tears, and she knew then that truth was the price she had to pay.

Ten

"So it's all been a lie?"

Unable to meet her grandfather's shocked blue eyes, Sarah Ann scuffed her sandaled feet on the warped, weathered boards of Angel's Landing's dock. Staring out across the peaceful, sun-kissed waters of Paradise Bay, she nodded miserably. "I'm afraid so. I'm sorry, Gramps."

"God almighty, girlie." From his seat on a flat-topped piling where he'd come to drink his mid-morning coffee, Harlan gazed at her in utter bewilderment. "What were you thinking?"

Folding her hands around her own coffee mug for strength, Sarah Ann wondered how she could answer that. Nervous perspiration dotted her upper lip and dripped between her breasts beneath the purple knit shirt she wore with her jeans. Confession was supposed to be good for the soul, but she'd never felt so small, so utterly contemptible, her explanations weak and venal and inexcusable.

She'd told Gramps everything, from her first outrageous proposal to Gabe Thornton, the planned subterfuge—so simple and innocent a thing, really—then the legal
mixup, the conflicts, her joy at Harlan's recovery, the fear
of being caught in this lie, the growing complications of her
deceit, even about the arson, and finally her decision to tell
all as the only honorable way out of this untenable predic-
ment.

The only thing she couldn't, wouldn't tell her grandfather was the intimate details of her affair with Gabe, how
he captivated her with a single look, a fleeting touch, and
how much she wanted him still. The way Gabe had held her
throughout the night proved that he wanted her, too, at
least in the physical sense. But he didn't love her, and she
would not try to bind him with sex any more than she'd
want him to stay in their farce of a marriage out of a misguided sense of duty or the fondness he felt for Harlan or
the place he'd made for himself on the farm and in their
lives.

No, she loved Gabe too much to let him make that kind
of sacrifice, only to lose him to regret and bitterness when
he inevitably realized the mistake he'd made. She'd sensed
that he was on the verge of just such a decision after he'd
made love to her last night, when she'd been so weak and
foolish as to confess her true feelings. But he'd risen at
dawn and left her to go about his investigation without
giving her an opportunity to dissuade him of that wrong-
headed notion.

The coffee in her mug was as black as the despair that
gripped her soul, but Sarah Ann knew she couldn't stoop
to manipulation, playing on Gabe's guilt because he'd
taken what she so willingly offered. Knowing how forceful
he was when he made up his mind, however, and knowing
her own weakness, she couldn't take any chances.

So she'd taken the choice away from both of them [
telling Gramps the truth.

She gave a small, helpless shrug. "What can I say?
thought you were dying, and I wanted to make your la
days happy."

"With such a lie?" Harlan shook his head. "I broug
you up better."

Shame filled her, stained her cheeks crimson. "That's n
the worst of it. I did it to keep you from selling out, too
was afraid, Gramps, afraid of losing you and my home.'

Harlan splashed the dregs of his coffee into the wa
lapping beneath the dock, shaking his head. "I nev
dreamed you were so desperate."

"It was wrong of me, I know that. But now that you'
stronger, I had to tell you the truth."

"Don't look so worried, girlie. This isn't going to cau
me to relapse. I'm made of sterner stuff than that, I
gum."

"Yes." She blew out a shaky breath, trying to smil
"I'm very glad to hear it."

Harlan's shaggy brows lowered in concern. "But wh
about Gabe? The two of you together—I'm not blind, y
know."

A sharp ache pierced her chest. "Gabe is a decent m
who deserves his freedom."

"You're in love with him, girlie."

She blinked on a sudden sting of tears, unable to deny
but determined to make things clear. "That doesn't ma
ter. He never bargained for any of this. We were both a
ing out a role, but that's over now, and the sooner we g
back to our own lives, the better for us all. It's what
wants, what he needs. I can't do less than give it to him.'

"Yes, I see." Harlan chewed his lower lip. "It chang
things back again, is all, his not being around to count on

"I understand."

"With everything gone wrong—" he waved his gnarled hand in a vague, encompassing gesture "—we're going to be hard-pressed to hold on, ain't we, girlie? Even worse than before."

"Yes."

He reached out and took her hand. "It's not the kind of life I want for you."

"I know that, Gramps. You deserve a rest, too."

"So there's only one answer."

Her stomach plummeted with a sinking sensation of loss, but she gathered her courage and ignored it. Swallowing hard, knowing this was merely a portion of the price to be paid for her sins, she squeezed Harlan's hand.

"I'll go call Douglas right now."

"She's gone. They both are."

"What the hell—?" Gabe came up short on the shell walkway, his concentration broken by the lazy announcement from the Amazon overloading his favorite hammock. "I told her to stay put!"

A curl of cigarette smoke drifted toward the cerulean dome of a cloudless afternoon sky. Rocking slightly in the rope contraption, Beulah gave Gabe a Cheshire Cat smile and wiggled her stubby toes, slapping her foam rubber flip-flops against her soles. "Since when does Sarah Ann take orders from a fool?"

"Don't you start in on me," Gabe snapped, whipping off his sunglasses. "I've got enough problems."

"No luck?"

"I didn't say that." Thinking about what he and Mike had learned made his eyes narrow and his jaw tighten in a deadly fashion that had once made bloodthirsty mercenaries plan early retirement. It was quite surprising what a lit-

tle knowledgeable poking around by a seasoned intelligenc
specialist could uncover, and Mike was one of the best i
the business.

But was it too much to ask a mere hundred-pound fe
male to follow orders for her own safety? Apparently
was. Gabe ground his molars and thought about beating:
then revised the vision to a more pleasurable form of pur
ishment. Yeah, when he got his hands on Sarah Ann agair
there'd be a reckoning. He looked forward to it.

"Did she tell you where she was going?" he demanded

"Nope."

"When she'd be back?"

"Nope."

Exasperated, Gabe hooked his sunglasses into his colla
"Well, what the devil did she say?"

"Not a damn thing. Just took her stuff and her grandp
and vamoosed like a lady with business to tend to."

Gabe scowled. "Hell."

Beulah scratched her bushy henna-red head and squinte
up at the clouds. "Yup, you got a real way with womer
Gabriel. Expecting us to read your mind, taking us fo
granted, playing little dishonest games...."

He shot her a suspicious look. "What's that supposed
mean?"

"Only that you can't get something for nothing these
days."

"You're talking nonsense. Look, I've got to track dow
Sarah—"

"You'd best do more than that, dogface." Beulah too
a drag on her cigarette and flicked the butt into the bushe
"If you plan to keep her, that is."

Gabe's jaw clenched. "This is none of your business."

"Rather go into battle naked than tell that gal you lov
her, huh? Maybe you're right about yourself—no guts."

Pricked to his most vulnerable core, Gabe's anger exploded. "Shut up, you damned harpy! What the hell do you know?"

With an air of dismissal, she crossed her beefy arms under her head and closed her eyes. "That Sarah Ann deserves better."

Beulah's blunt words and the sure knowledge that they were absolutely true sent Gabe's temper over the edge. "You go straight to hell!"

Beulah smiled. "Been there. Done that. Don't recommend it, neither."

Maddened, Gabe mouthed a string of expletives, turned on his boot heel and stormed off.

"Hey, Cap'n?"

"What!" He cast a furious glare over his shoulder at the figure in the hammock and caught a shimmer of alabaster radiance out of the corner of his eye.

Swinging around in consternation, he blinked, but there was nothing but Beulah, watching him with a mocking expression. He scowled, trying to re-create in his mind what he'd seen—thought he'd seen?—in that infinitesimal instant. A trick of the light? For the briefest of eye blinks, he could have sworn there'd been a countenance of celestial beauty superimposed over Beulah's ugly mug, someone he strained to remember and recognize, his guide through a green hell when life had been unsure....

Like waking from a dream, the ephemeral certitude dissolved, forgotten in a single dizzy moment. The harder he tried to hold it, the quicker it slipped away, like clutching mist between his fingers. Unsure where his fantastic thoughts had taken him, Gabe shook his head, shedding the moment of vertigo, recalled to his mission.

"I'm going to find Sarah Ann. Keep her here if she comes back, okay?"

She snorted. "You think she's got something to come back to? More fool you, but life's a risk, ain't it?"

"No funny business, Beulah. I mean it!" He turned to go.

"Sure. Whatever you say, Gabriel. Best remember one thing, though."

"Yeah?"

Beulah's black eyes pierced him, their usual mischief replaced by something that in another, less-recalcitrant individual might have been compassion, even affection.

"Sarah Ann ain't wrong about you."

"As difficult as your decision has been, Harlan, I know you can't go wrong with this plan."

Douglas Ritchie's unctuous tone held just the right amount of concern and conviction to be reassuring, but Sarah Ann could find no comfort in it. Nerves stretched taut, unable to relax enough to sit, she hovered near her grandfather, taking in the plush details of Douglas's private office—hardwood floors and Persian rugs, a wall of civic awards and a bookshelf of Boehm porcelain birds.

"Seems we got no choice." Dwarfed by the massive wing chair pulled up before Douglas's acre-wide office desk, Harlan shrugged. "If not for your offer—"

"Glad I'm able to help out. You know that." His manner hearty, Douglas leaned back in his leather swivel chair, peering through his spectacles and rubbing his thumb back and forth over the edge of a thin manila folder. "The affection I feel for both of you can't be measured in terms of money. Now, if you want to just look over this option before you sign . . ."

"When I called, I never expected things to move so fast," Sarah Ann said, feeling rather bowled over.

Douglas's cordiality and eagerness to be of assistance had
een almost overwhelming, his helpfulness and determi-
ation that they take care of this rather unpleasant busi-
ess as quickly as possible—today, this afternoon—
ordering on insistence. Sarah Ann knew it was probably
etter this way. She and Gramps had made the decision,
nd there'd be no going back. A quick resolution to the
ituation and the chance to move on would be the most
ainless solution.

"It was merely a matter of Angie's filling in some blanks
n the standard forms." Douglas fingered the knot of his
e, a faint sheen of perspiration coating his upper lip even
ough the room was pleasantly cool. Opening the folder,
e pushed pages of legal documents across the desk to
arlan. "Now, if you'll look here, you'll see we've ex-
uded the tract where the house sits, of course. The rest of
e property goes for the standard per-acre sum—"

Harlan picked up the first page, shaking his wispy head.
Barely clear the debts, but it's better than throwing more
ood money after bad, I suppose. You got a pen, Doug-
s?"

Breaking into a smile, Douglas whipped a fat Mont Blanc
ountain pen out of his coat and presented it to the old man
s if it were King Arthur's Excaliber. "Absolutely.
ere—"

"Sure you really want to do this, Harlan?"

Three heads swiveled at the sound of Gabe's rumbled
uestion. He stood in the doorway, the tip of one boot
ropped over the other instep, swinging his sunglasses by
e stem, the picture of indolence. But it was a deceptive
lm, Sarah Ann knew with immediate alarm, for his tawny
redator's eyes burned, and his stance held the leashed
nsion of a lion ready to pounce.

"Gabe." She took a little breath. "What are you doin
here?"

"Looking for you, sweetheart." His mouth com
pressed. "We're going to have a little talk later about fo
lowing orders. Luckily, in Lostman's Island about twent
people saw the direction you went."

Douglas surged to his feet, his expression laced with grir
annoyance. "This is a private meeting, Mr. Thornton.
suggest you—"

"Since apparently it concerns my wife's inheritance, I'
say I have a vested interest in what's going down," Gab
drawled.

A bolt of defiance tilted Sarah Ann's chin. "It's nc
necessary to continue the charade, Gabriel. I've tol
Gramps everything."

Lifting a sandy eyebrow, Gabe stepped into the offic
"That so?"

"Yes. *Everything.*"

"Made it right, did you?" Admiration reverberated i
the husky timbre of his voice. "That's damned coura
geous."

"It's time to end the lies."

"Time for a little trust, too," he murmured, almost 1
himself.

Somewhat taken aback, Sarah Ann gripped the back c
Harlan's chair for support, her knuckles white, and u
tered the hardest thing she'd ever had to say. "So there's n
question now. You're released of all responsibilities. You'
free."

"I know you wish it were that easy, darlin'."

Rattled by the warmth that kindled behind his eyes, sh
fought down a sense of desperation. Didn't he unde
stand? What good was her telling the truth if he refused 1
take advantage of it?

"Look here, Gabe," Harlan said, his puckish features screwed into a picture of puzzlement, "Sarah Ann told me you wanted out of all this."

"Sarah Ann's been known to be mistaken."

His words stunned her, sent panic rushing through her veins.

"Don't you do this to me!" she said furiously. "I won't have a man in my life for all the wrong reasons, do you hear? Gramps, we've got no other choice. Sign those papers so we can go."

Swift, efficient and helpful, Douglas spread the documents on the edge of the desk. "Perhaps that would be best. We can sort out details later. I know you've been under tremendous pressure, what with all your financial worries, and now this arson is such a dreadful shock, but just think of this as a solution that will relieve the strain—"

Trying to ignore Gabe, Sarah Ann watched Harlan fumble to uncap the fountain pen, her mind spinning. They were actually going to sell the place, and then it would be all over, so Gabe could have his freedom, and her life truly would be nothing but ashes, but—

"Wait, Gramps." She closed her fingers over the stem of the pen, frowning across the desk at Douglas. "I never said anything about arson, Douglas. How did you know about that?"

Looking faintly flustered, the Realtor shrugged. "Must have heard it in town. You know how word gets around. Be sure to sign all four copies, Harlan."

"No." She plucked the pen free of her grandfather's gnarled fingers and flung it on the desktop. "Who told you, Douglas? Gabe and his partners and Gramps and I are the only ones who knew the fire was set."

Moisture dotted Douglas's upper lip, but he kept his tone reasonable, placating. "I'm certain you mentioned it, Sarah Ann."

"I'm sure I didn't. Why are you lying?"

"Maybe it's a disease," Gabe offered mildly.

"You stay out of this, Thornton!" Douglas's face turned ruddy with choler. "You've caused Sarah Ann nothing but misery."

"Maybe so, and maybe you and I are more alike than I'd like to admit, since I traded services for a piece of frontage. But at least I never lied to her, never wooed her and the old man just to get my hands on their property. Would you really have married her to get it?"

"You don't know what you're talking about. I've simply been a friend." Douglas dug for a handkerchief and mopped his face.

Gabe's lips twisted. "Yeah, a real pal. A friend who never quite got around to mentioning the new citrus processing plant in the works and the fact their number one choice of location is the Dempsey place."

"What?" Stunned, Sarah Ann stared.

"It's not exactly an inspired setup," Gabe said, "but it works well enough. Buy at rock bottom from desperate owners and sell high under the table to a well-heeled conglomerate. From what Mike uncovered about the sorry state of your *pal's* overextended finances, it would take a deal of this size to bail him out. When I came on the scene, he had to figure out a new way to make you desperate enough to sell out."

"This is slander!" Douglas blustered. "Sarah Ann, don't believe a word!"

Gabe crossed his arms, his smile mocking. "Of course, by the time the Feds get through with you for all your shady practices, Ritchie, it won't really matter that you conspired to commit arson as well."

"This is absurd. You can't prove a thing!"

Gabe's eyes gleamed. "Give it time. I've got a couple of friends working on that."

The way Douglas blanched told Sarah Ann all she needed to know. "Damn you, Douglas! You arranged that fire to force us to sell, didn't you? And the rest of it—you're on the bank board so a well-placed word from you and they denied our loan. And the property assessments? Oh, hell, you lied about that, too!"

Gabe slanted her an admiring look. "You're damned quick on the uptake, sweetheart."

Harlan struggled to his feet, his lined face as pugnacious as a bulldog's. "You swindling, lying scumbag! Wait'll I get my hands on you—"

"Never mind, Gramps." Livid, Sarah Ann grabbed the option documents, ripped them in half and threw them at Douglas. He flinched and ducked as the torn papers fluttered over the desktop and onto the floor. Her lip curled with disdain. "Sorry, Douglas, but we have to decline your kind offer."

"You're making a big mistake," he warned, "taking his word over mine."

"I don't think so. Some men know the meaning of honor."

At her unspoken inference Douglas's facade of innocence snapped, and his expression went cold. "Suit yourself, but you'll regret this, I guarantee it."

"Be kind of hard to carry out threats from a jail cell, won't it?" Gabe asked, his own smile deadly.

"Get out."

"No problem. Come on, Sarah, Harlan." Gabe began to usher them toward the door. "The stench in here was getting to me, anyway."

His countenance purple, Douglas spewed his frustration. "At least I wasn't stupid enough to actually marry this whey-faced old maid!"

With an angry hiss, Gabe's affability vanished, and he lunged, grabbed Douglas by the collar and raised his fist.

"Gabe, no!" Sarah Ann clutched at his arm, forestalling the blow. "He's not worth it."

The furious blaze in Gabe's eyes flickered, and his jaw twitched, then he shoved Douglas away with unconcealed contempt. "Just watch what you say about my wife, you bastard."

Douglas straightened his tie, sneering. "You gutless wonder, I'll have the law on you for assault—aughh!"

Sarah Ann's punch landed in Douglas's stomach with such force he windmilled backward, out of balance, and slammed into the bookcase. Plaques tumbled from the shelves and a ceramic owl and two eagles smashed to smithereens. Winded and green, Douglas doubled over and slid to the floor, flinching as a framed Realtor of the Year certificate landed in his lap.

Feet spread among the rubble, fists on hips, Sarah Ann glared down at him. "Assault *that,* Douglas. And watch what the hell you call my husband!"

Gabe gazed at her in awed amazement. "My God, you're a formidable woman."

"Let's get out of here."

Head high, Sarah Ann marched Harlan and Gabe past the baffled receptionist and out of the office into the late afternoon somnolence of Lostman's Island's main street. By the time she crossed the palm-lined asphalt parking lo to her truck, and found Gabe's Jeep neatly tucked in beside it, she was shaking with reaction.

"To think that boy was out to gull us all along," Harlan muttered, shaking his head. "Girlie, I should have paid more attention to you."

"I bought his blarney, too, Gramps." Folding her arms to hide her trembling, she stopped beside the Jeep and turned to face Gabe. "I don't know how you uncovered everything, but thank you, Gabriel."

"All part of the service, ma'am. And if you and Harlan are willing to deal with the processing plant folks, I think the problems with the farm will be over. Be a good use for those damaged orchards, not to mention a boost to the local economy."

Sarah Ann knew she should be elated over that news, but somehow it didn't seem as important anymore.

"What about Douglas?" Harlan demanded. "He's not going to get away with this scot-free, is he?"

Gabe shook his head. "Not a chance. He's up to his eyeballs in trouble with irate investors and federal regulators. The indictments for fraud ought to come down within days. His troubles are just beginning."

"Then that just leaves you and the girlie to sort things out." Ignoring the way Sarah Ann's face flamed, Harlan cocked an inquisitive eyebrow at Gabe. "Think you want to keep her?"

"Damn straight I do."

"You'll take care of her?"

"You have my hand on it."

Gabe and Harlan shook hands on the pact with due solemnity.

Sarah Ann looked on, openmouthed with chagrin and outrage. Finally, she found her voice. "Just who do you two think you are, arranging my life for me?"

"Sarah—"

"Girlie—"

"No!" She struck her fist against her chest. "*I'm* ir charge of my own life. Me! When I thought the ranch wa: gone, I realized it isn't the Dempsey legacy that makes m who I am. I'm a worthwhile person, and I can do what ever I need to do by myself."

"Maybe I'll wait in the truck," Harlan announced grinning. Neither Gabe nor Sarah Ann paid any attentior as he went around to the other vehicle.

"Get this straight, Gabe Thornton," Sarah Ann saic furiously, "I don't need you to take care of me!"

"You said you love me."

She caught her breath. "I do, but I've got more prid than to live with a man on sufferance or out of pity. I de serve to find happiness on my own terms."

Gabe clasped Sarah Ann's upper arms, drawing her re sisting form close. His voice was husky with emotion. "S name your terms, ma'am."

Startled, she looked up into her gentle warrior's golde eyes, and a thrill of hope darted through her at what sh saw stirring there. All her life, out of loyalty and love, she' placed everyone else's needs above her own dreams. But he experience with Gabe had taught her something about he own worth, about having the courage to ask for what sh needed—even deserved—for a change. Dared she risk it? I she didn't, how could she live with herself?

Licking her lips, she made her demand. "I want it al Unconditional surrender."

"Done. As long as it's for life."

She trembled, wanting to believe, but wary. "As easy a that?"

"Hell, no, it's not easy to a man like me to change, but got no choice!"

"No choice?" Baffled confusion clouded her eyes. "Why?"

"Because I'm crazy in love with you, lady, can't you tell?" He cupped her face, his fingers stroking her cheeks. "You captured my heart, turned me inside out from the very start, only I've been too stubborn and too scared to admit it."

"Oh." Awe at this miracle made her tremulous. "Are you sure?"

"I was empty and you filled me up. How can I go back to the emptiness? You talk of pity, but I'm the one who needs it. I'm so damned terrified I'll mess up, but if you believe in me, maybe I'm not so bad."

"No," she whispered, touching his face, "you're not so bad."

"Let's do it, then—marriage, family, farm—the whole shooting match. We'll make a life of it together." His grin was lopsided, unsure—and melted her heart. "You have to admit it'll resolve a lot of problems."

She stiffened. "If that's the only reason—"

His kiss silenced her protest, liquified her spine. When he lifted his head, they were both breathing hard. "What do you think?"

"You do love me." Wonder shone in her violet eyes.

"Didn't I say that? I know I'm no bargain, but I'm willing to risk it if you are." Smiling, he ran his fingers through the springy curls at her temple. "Only this time, let's do it the old-fashioned way."

"How?"

"I need a wife, Sarah Ann Dempsey. I need a woman who'll fight with me and hold me in the dead of night when I shake and love me in every way there is until death do us part. I need *you*. This time, I'm asking you—will you marry me?"

"Yes!" She threw her arms around his neck, joyous and giddy. "Yes, of course I will."

"Thank God."

The shudder that shook him told her he hadn't been completely certain of her answer, and he tightened his arms around her, an embrace that was protective and possessive and utterly thrilling to Sarah Ann. The willingness of this strong man to show her his vulnerabilities filled her with the surety that their love, their friendship, their intimacy would grow and blossom for a future of unimaginable brightness.

"We've been blessed," she said, touching his sun-streaked hair, healing his scars with loving fingers. "Someone up there must be watching out for us."

Gabe jerked, startled, and a plethora of emotions chased across his lean features—curiosity, wonder, acceptance, faith.

"You know, sweetheart," he said slowly, "I think you might be right."

And then Gabriel Thornton kissed his wife again, in full view of heaven and the whole town of Lostman's Island.

Inside the truck, watching the goings-on through the rearview mirror, Harlan grinned to himself and contemplated life, love and great-grandchildren.

Epilogue

"The sign clearly states this is a no-smoking section."

"What sign?" Though it tried, the raucous voice could in no way sound innocent.

After a long moment a small plaque encrusted with scrolled golden lettering rematerialized. "That sign."

"Uh-huh."

Wind whispered on a celestial sigh. "Back to the report."

"I got it done, didn't I? Have a look-see if you don't believe me—The Cap'n and his lady are having a heckuva belated honeymoon at that overpriced bed-and-breakfast."

"Voyeurism is not condoned in these regions."

A shrug. "Stuffy rulc, if you ask me."

"Your charge would not be amused."

"Hey, now that he's got his lady to watch over him, Gabriel and me got an understanding. You see the way he

jumped all over Michael when that red-headed scoundre
tried to fire my a—"

"Swearing is prohibited, too, I'll remind you. An
Mike's anger was certainly justified after what you did t
him."

The raspy chuckle contained a wealth of malicious an
ticipation. "Time to teach that Irishman a thing or two."

"Then pay attention. As usual, while the end results wer
satisfactory, your methods are totally suspect."

"What's wrong with 'em?"

"Bullying an old man, swigging beer with those yahoo:
and your carelessness! It's not the first time Gabriel nearl
saw—"

"But he didn't, so don't get your knickers in an up
roar."

A little shocked pause. "Knickers—or my lack of them—
is not the issue. Your meddling is."

"That's my job, ain't it?"

"Identifying too closely with your charges is not. We'v
warned you, humanity is dangerous. You're becoming quit
disgracefully corrupted!"

"Rule Number 202— 'Personal risk is of no considera
tion when the mission is at stake.'"

"That phony holier-than-thou attitude doesn't fl
around here, especially since we know how much you'v
always relished—excuse the term—*hell-raising* with thos
three boys."

"Sorry. But I only got two to go now."

"So go. But no more cheating at cards, and watch th
cursing, and *try* to stay out of trouble this time!"

"Ain't no fun that way."

"I beg your pardon?"

"Nothing. Just thinking about the two hard-heads I've got to tend to until my replacements show up." The husky words were already fading. "Lots to do. Gotta go."

"Godspeed, then..." Another long-suffering sigh whispered on the breeze. "And for St. Pete's sake, try to give up smoking!"

*   *   *   *   *

SILHOUETTE® Desire®

COMING NEXT MONTH

#1045 THE COFFEEPOT INN—Lass Small

January's *Man of the Month*, Bryan Willard, met the most alluring female he'd ever seen—who turned out to be his new boss. He agreed to show inexperienced Lily Trevor the ropes...but he hadn't planned on teaching her about love!

#1046 BACHELOR MOM—Jennifer Greene

The Stanford Sisters

Single mother Gwen Stanford's secret birthday wish was to have a wild romance. But when her handsome neighbor Spense McKenna offered to give her just that, was Gwen *truly* ready to throw caution to the wind and succumb to Spense's seductive charms?

#1047 THE TENDER TRAP—Beverly Barton

One night of uncontrollable passion between old-fashioned Adam Wyatt and independent Blythe Elliott produced a surprise bundle of joy. They married for the sake of the baby, but would these expectant parents find true love?

#1048 THE LONELIEST COWBOY—Pamela Macaluso

Rancher Clint Slade's immediate attraction to devoted single mother Skye Williamson had him thinking that she might be the woman to ease his lonely heart. But would Skye's six-year-old secret destroy their future happiness?

#1049 RESOLVED TO (RE) MARRY—Carole Buck

Holiday Honeymoons

After eleven years, ex-spouses Lucy Falco and Christopher Banks were thrown together by chance on New Year's Eve. It didn't take long before they discovered how steamy their passion still was....

#1050 ON WINGS OF LOVE—Ashley Summers

Katy Lawrence liked to play it safe, while pilot Thomas Logan preferred to take risks. Could Thomas help Katy conquer her fears and persuade her to gamble on love?

A Funny Thing Happened on the Way to the Baby Shower...

When four college friends reunite to celebrate the arrival of one bouncing baby, they find four would-be grooms on the way!

Don't miss a single, sexy tale in

RAYE MORGAN'S

Only in

BABY DREAMS
in May '96 (SD #997)

A GIFT FOR BABY
in July '96 (SD #1010)

BABIES BY THE BUSLOAD
in September '96 (SD #1022)

And look for

INSTANT DAD, WILL TRAIN
in November '96

Only from

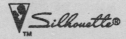

RMBS

SILHOUETTE® *Desire*

He's the sexiest hero around...and he's waiting for you in a red-hot romance created by your favorite top authors....

He's Silhouette Desire's MAN OF THE MONTH!

Don't miss a single one of these incredibly irresistible hunks—

In January	**THE COFFEEPOT INN** by **Lass Small**	
In February	**TEXAS MOON** by **Joan Elliott Pickart**	
In March	**TIGHT-FITTIN' JEANS** by **Mary Lynn Baxter**	
In April	**LUCY AND THE LONER** by **Elizabeth Bevarly**	
In May	**WHO'S THE BOSS?** by **Barbara Boswell**	
In June	**THE UNFORGETABLE MAN** by **Joan Hohl**	

And later this year, watch for sizzling stories by some of your other favorite authors— Diana Palmer, Ann Major, Cait London and Dixie Browning!

MAN OF THE MONTH...ONLY FROM SILHOUETTE DESIRE

MOM97JJ

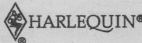